I0607840

DÉJÀ VU

AND THE

PHONE SEX QUEEN

by

Michael McIrvin

Fearful Symmetry Publications

This book is a work of fiction. Names, characters, places and incidents are the product of the author's imagination or are used fictitiously. Any resemblance to actual locales, events, or persons, living or dead, is coincidental.

Copyright (c) 2002, 2020 by Michael McIrvin. All rights reserved. No part of this publication may be reproduced, stored in a retrieval system, or transmitted, in any form or by any means, electronic, mechanical, photocopying, recording or otherwise, without the prior written permission of the publisher.

Fearful Symmetry Publications edition: 2020

First published: J-Press Publishing, 2002
Printed in the United States of America.

Third printing
10 9 8 7 6 5 4 3 2 1

Library of Congress Control Number: 2001093262

ISBN 978-1-7341970-6-8

Fearful Symmetry Publications

Cover image by Julio Aldana

Part One

I will a round unvarnished tale deliver
Of my whole course of love-what drugs, what charms,
What conjuration, and what mighty magic...

—William Shakespeare, *Othello*, Act I, Scene III

Chapter 1

Zeke Reilly used to flirt with his mother-in-law. Nothing dangerous. A pinch on the cheek, a wink like they had an inside joke. But there was always a subtle sexual overtone in their interaction, like the muted roar of a wild river under the ground, like there was a raging desire between them but buried deep under layers of social convention and surrounded by thick stone walls of taboo. Like, what could happen if...rippled through every hello, every smile.

But those monolithic walls never actually shook much, let alone crumble, and the tectonic plates of convention held solid over the torrent underneath. Aside from their small flirtations nothing in his socially sanctioned relationship with Judy slipped, even a little, except in his dreams.

At least in Zeke's dreams things were different, but then everything is different in the quagmire of the subconscious, or so he told himself mornings after Judy's apparitional caresses had jolted through every corpuscle in his body and he awoke exhausted and sweating.

His mother-in-law had a different view of dreams and other like products of the human psyche. She had told Zeke several times that his dreams and waking premonitions and déjà vu experiences, experiences he'd tried to ignore since he was nine, were a natural function of the spirit, *spiritus* she called it.

"That portion of you that comes from God but that precedes even Him," she said, "that is more than merely eternal as in been-around-forever...more like always-was in the sense of always-will-be."

Judy liked such language, convoluted and strange, no matter how remotely spiritual or philosophical the subject. For Judy the price of vegetables or the barometric pressure or a flea market could be the inspiration for existential and phenomenal discourse. Such language alternately embarrassed Zeke, especially if he'd had concupiscent dreams recently, confused him, made him nauseous, amazed him, or made him nearly swoon with affection for the tiny redheaded woman out of whose mouth the words swam like fish, flew like birds, galloped like wild sweat-soaked horses with rippling muscles. His reaction tended to depend on where his own psychic barometer was on that given day.

Today he just wanted to hear Judy's voice, to watch her throat move gently as she talked, to imagine her lips doing magic tricks to his penis like he had dreamt the night before.

"It seems so strange to you, to us all on those rare occasions it happens to most of us," she said, "because of our limited apprehension, you might even say our misapprehension, of time. Time is a simultaneity, not a river flowing from some unknowable source to some unknowable terminus. It is multitudinous possibility that we all sample in our dreams but explain away as some kind of psychological detritus, as meaningless interference in our normal, as in waking and rational, consciousness."

Pictures of Judy's mouth moving over him from his dreams the previous night flashed through Zeke's imagination like his own personal pornographic movie. He could feel his ears growing red hot, the electric tingle in his pants.

"And some few, like you Zeke, sample time, investigate the possibilities, while walking around, or sitting at the table, or driving to work."

"Or pooping," Zeke joked, trying to hide his embarrassment. "Some people read *Time* magazines on the pot, some visit the beyond." He winked at Judy across the table. At that moment there was a rumbling in Zeke's inner ear like far off thunder. The sky out Judy's kitchen window began to swirl over the Rocky Mountains.

6

The mountains themselves began to swirl. This was prelude to a vision, but Zeke pretended it wasn't happening. Sometimes he could hold off the experience, the disconcerting shift in consciousness, if he pretended hard enough it wasn't happening. Sometimes, inevitable as rain, nothing stopped it, and his being was flooded with sensory information all jumbled together but also heightened beyond what he saw or heard or smelled normally. Normal, he thought, Judy might ridicule the notion, but he longed for the status quo of everyday mind, for this sensory disruption to fade.

He could hear Marianne whistling Bach in her mother's bathroom over the din in his head. She'd been fixing her hair for twenty minutes, probably listening to their conversation. She'd noticed the way Zeke looked at her mother and even accused him once of lusting after her in his heart, a phrase she'd borrowed from a former president of the United States. He'd told her she was crazy, that he was just very fond of their conversations, though he knew she didn't completely buy it and watched and listened closer now.

Marianne must have grown tired of listening to them talk today, or just knew the conversation was over, like usual, when Zeke said something he intended to be funny to take the edge off his own uneasiness, to lighten the mystical subject, but that always came out silly, trivial.

Marianne was whistling mightily now, one of the Brandenburg Concertos. Zeke didn't know Bach well enough to know which one.

She had the unique ability to whistle contrapuntally, which made her renditions of Bach almost dazzling. She said it had something to do with the gap between her upper incisors, but she never explained her talent to him beyond that, or probably to herself. Marianne was her mother's antithesis.

When they first met seven years before, she used to whistle in bed after sex. Zeke knew then the sex was just so-so, and it

7

remained so-so to this very morning's slap-dash before he showered and shaved, but the music added enough, somehow, to make it adequate. Marianne only whistled once in a while now, and never after sex.

Judy was putting water on for tea. Zeke was sorry she stopped talking. Today, he loved her abstraction. It reminded him of Yeats' poetry. He was reading the Collected Shorter Poems between customers at the bookstore where he was the night clerk. Besides, if she talked, the thunder and dizziness could be ignored a little more easily, if he had something else to focus on...

Zeke held his hand to his heart dramatically: "'Gaze no more on the phantoms, Niainh said, And kissed my eyes, and, swaying her bright head, And her bright body, sang of faery and man, Before God was or my old line began.'"

Judy folded her thin arms and smiled at him from where she stood before the stove. Zeke's blurred vision settled on the gray streaks at her temples that seemed to shimmer like lightning bolts, and the noise in his head grew louder.

"I might sing to you of the same things, something in Latin to match Marianne's ecstatic whistling." She nodded toward the bathroom. Marianne was racing up and down the minor scales two steps at a time like the world's fastest human would take stairs.

"But I wouldn't recommend not looking at what only you can see."

The thunder in Zeke's inner ear began to subside and the dizziness was nearly gone. He'd managed to hold the vision off, whatever it was, by ignoring it, for the time being.

"When the very heart strings of God quiver," Judy said, "and another possible world dances into focus, it could be damned dangerous not to pay very close attention."

Chapter 2

Zeke made no claim, indeed made no effort, to understand his strange sensations, his aching knowledge that something was about to happen, or his almost continual sensation of having been, wherever he happened to be, before.

As a child in Brooklyn the experience merely frightened him. At age nine he'd dreamt every night for a week that a train jumped the tracks at the bridge two blocks from his house and several cars plunged to the street below. That Friday he had skipped school and stood within sight of the bridge. He didn't have to wait long. At 9:12 a.m. a drunken engineer nose-dived his engine and six cars onto the road, killing himself, several passengers, and two longhaired guys in a V.W. bus unlucky enough to be on the road just under the train track at 9:12 a.m. on a Friday. They had disappeared before Zeke's eyes like in a cartoon: click-click-click, ding-ding-ding, a crash and a splat and sparks flying, and two guys in a micro-bus were flat as pancakes.

Zeke was almost in shock at first, as the smoke billowed up from the V.W.'s exploded gas tank, as sirens sounded and lights flashed. He thought he had caused this mayhem, but something in his nine year old mind dismissed the notion almost as it arose. He felt far too helpless before the dreams and the vision of them became real to be the cause of anything.

Besides, he tried experiments. He learned to program his dreams by thinking hard before he fell asleep of what he wanted to dream about. He purposely dreamt his father won at the track, the big one, the long odds, like in the movies. He dreamt his favorite Uncle Earl, who always told him scary stories and gave him crisp dollar bills, escaped from Attica where he'd languished two years for armed robbery. He dreamt he got to see his cousin Annie's bare

16 year old breasts from so close he could smell the bubble gum on her breath...

His dad never won anything more than an occasional two dollar bet, enough to get him stinking drunk once every month or so. His Uncle Earl did the remaining eight years of his sentence, then went back to Attica for life a year after that for killing his ex-wife. And all he ever saw of Annie's tits was the tight little crack between them where her swimsuit pushed them together at the annual family trek to Coney Island.

There were also more unsettling experiences. He dreamt he flunked 6th grade, and then did flunk 6th grade. He knew, before his older sister began to show any signs, that she was pregnant, that the father was Billy Sims, a black boy from Bedford-Stuyvesant, even though Jeanne insisted it was some sailor gone to sea, a white one, right up to the baby's birth when she subsequently confessed that Billy was the only boy with whom she'd ever had sex. He'd known Uncle Earl would look for Billy Sims and, though the rest of his family feared he'd kill the kid more for being black than for his paternity, that he'd like Billy immediately, get drunk with him on Mogen David wine and wish him all the luck in the world with tears in his eyes. He'd known that Uncle Earl would kill his ex-wife Mavis with a single punch when he found her in bed with some guy from Hoboken who happened to be a police detective and carrying a snub-nose .38 with which he would subdue Uncle Earl and hold him until the police arrived, that Earl would be weeping like a child for what he had done when they surrounded the place.

But with all this, Zeke made no attempt to figure out his prescience. For the most part he tried to ignore the experiences, to pretend they were dreams like other people have, that the sensory strangeness and the visions they accompanied were merely vertigo brought on by a build-up of fluid in his inner ear.

He'd told Judy about his experiences only because he'd had a vision in her presence one day and she accused him of being

10

drunk. His eyes had crossed, she said, and he fell over in her kitchen. So far, she was the only one in whose presence this had ever happened. Even Marianne thought he was merely prone to inexplicable headaches and dizziness, his migraines she called them.

He'd only lost control in front of another person that once and, because it was Judy, and because of how he felt about her, he couldn't stand her thinking anything negative about him. It was their secret. Though he knew Marianne listened in on their conversations when she could, he doubted she understood any of it. She had always maintained her mother was beyond her understanding, that Judy was a nut, as she put it, but anything Marianne did not understand she tended to discount as insanity. Besides Judy, poetry and Shakespeare and existential philosophy and seafood were also in the category, "crazy." Zeke was sure she had also filed him there a long time ago.

In spite of his discussions with Judy, or rather her attempts to make sense of his condition, he hadn't changed his approach much in dealing with it. He still pretended nothing was happening as best he could as his ears rang and he lost sense of time and place to varying degrees. He still told himself everything was all coincidence when the dreams and visions became the stuff of actual experience. In spite of all evidence to the contrary, this had been his strategy for dealing with his idiosyncrasy for 30 years.

There had been a subtle change over time, however. Incrementally, Zeke had begun to accept, if only a little, the validity of his prescience. Some part of him said, "coincidence"; some part merely accepted what was as what he somehow, at some level, knew would be. He lived in some nether region between denial and acceptance, that place where they are twins. Which is to say, though he could not wholly accept his experiences, Zeke even refused to think long or hard about them and very little surprised him anymore.

11

So the shock of Marianne's call was muted. He was rereading the same poem from Yeats he'd quoted to Judy and thinking about her with a proverbial lump in his throat, and an actual one in his pants, when the phone rang. Marianne wailed at him that her mother was dead, that she'd been hit by a furniture delivery truck as she jogged across a quiet street in the Denver suburb where she had lived since Marianne's father ran off with the baby-sitter 30 years before.

He'd told Judy his dream: Her tight little body lay twisted and bleeding under a street sign, Magnolia and 3rd. She was dressed in her black Lycra jogging suit. She wore a blood red bandanna around her auburn hair. A young man in a tee shirt knelt over her, held her in his arms her last minute on Earth.

"A Samaritan. It is comforting to know they are still with us," she had said.

"But if all you say is true," Zeke told her, surprised by her nonchalance, "then it isn't inevitable. You can change this. Just stay off that corner. Maybe quit jogging."

Judy had laughed. "You have misunderstood," she said.

Zeke didn't doubt that. Not only did he not always get all the conceptual stuff she threw at him, he didn't care. For him, their secret, his visions and dreams, had a sexual feel to it, like an affair but diminished to a more manageable size. He liked sharing this part of himself with her, but at the same time her concentration on it made him uneasy. He felt the embodiment of paradox: The secret they shared made him ache in that fine way arousal aches in the heart and loins, but her talking about it circumvented his only defense against his fear and uncertainty, circumvented his denial. Or at least he had to work far harder at it.

"This is one possible end in a sea of endings," Judy had said, and smiled at him in the way he had only believed lovers smiled. He had wanted to hold her, to sink to his knees and wrap his arms around her hips, to pull her tight to him.

12

"What if I do avoid that corner forever? What if I stop jogging and never wear black Lycra and a red bandanna? What will change? The place? The implement of my destruction? The time? And by how much?"

"So why am I supposed to pay so much attention to my dreams and waking visions?" he had asked. "If I can't change anything.

"But that's not what I'm suggesting," said Judy. "What you have witnessed is an ending. Mine. The how and the where can change, but an ending is an ending. Besides, it's not like you saw me shooting myself in despair, or dying of cancer because of some bad habit, some change I can will. What you saw was the hand of God."

"And the hand of God is shaped just like a ten-ton GMC with an overweight Hispanic man sporting a goatee at the wheel," Zeke said. He could not help himself.

****

Zeke had already felt the grief that swarmed through him like bees en masse as he knelt in St. Joseph's Cathedral, as the priest raised a silver chalice between his hands and said things he could not hear, already had not heard ten times or more in vision and in dream.

The real thing was geometrically larger than those previous versions, however. A thousand "what ifs" lay like a rock in his stomach, and he longed to sob like Marianne sobbed beside him, in long, rolling explosions of his transmuted desire that had turned to something inside him black as bile, let loose on the air.

What if she had not merely smiled like an angel when he told her what he'd seen of her death? What if she were just a little bit less Catholic and would have tried to escape 3rd and Magnolia, maybe fled with him to Mexico, somewhere? What if he had met Judy before he met her daughter, the contrapuntal whistler?

13

He could hear Marianne's slight two-toned whistle now as she exhaled, the same small music she made in her sleep. Then he felt the flutter of wings in his chest and his throat, the roll of thunder deep in his ears. He strained to ignore it, but his sight began to fade, or rather all images became a single morass of color until he saw the molecules themselves spinning and darting like frightened fish. All noise became a single low- pitched hum, and all smells-his own sweat, Marianne's strident perfume, candle wax and incense and human grief (which smells like the ocean, its margin where what dies rots, but also its pure depths)-became a single smell.

Then there was a flash of brilliant light, and another, and Zeke found himself standing next to Marianne and the priest was speaking again. Zeke could hear him now, every word, even over Marianne's growing noise, and he could see him as if looking through binoculars. He could see the priest's eyelids quiver as he intoned with his eyes half closed, the bead of sweat on his lip, small drops of spit flying.

Clearest of all were the smells, an odd synthesis, but separable, identifiable, though Zeke could locate no source for them in the church. He smelled roses, sex, popcorn, and scorched butter.

Chapter 3

There are things Cindy Sweet simply cannot imagine, cannot conjure a picture of no matter how hard she tries. Like Andy Warhol with an erection, or Jean Paul Sartre at the breakfast table in his boxer shorts telling the maid jokes about Catholics. Like herself, happy.

These were exercises with which she tried to improve her imagination, something Danny, her first husband, said she lacked.

14

He told her almost every day, from the time they met in a bar in L.A. when she was on vacation until their divorce, that nothing can change if you can't see the possibilities. Unless you try on alternatives with your mind, he liked to say, you are destined to die where and what you are this very minute.

In the year since the divorce was final she had become more and more sure he was right. Not only are the imagination-less doomed, but she was imagination-less. This realization went a long way toward explaining her life, especially the last twelve months of it.

Right after they signed the papers Danny had left town with all of what little money was in the bank, in violation of the divorce decree that said they were to split it down the middle. Then she lost her job taking pictures at weddings for a big photography studio. Then the small house she and Danny had bought two years before, which was supposed to be sold and any profit split, and which she thought was now all hers since Danny's exit with the savings, was repossessed when she could not make the payments and no one wanted to buy it.

Last week her ten year old Subaru quit on I-25 during rush hour traffic never to be revived, with a major backfire and a billowing cloud of black smoke, and last month Zig had made an early exit from her life.... The list of losses was a long one, and she simply could not imagine anything else. Life was just this-subtraction.

So right after Zig's disappearance she had taken up trying to improve her imagination with these simple exercises. Every morning she lay naked on her couch in the convenience apartment at the edge of Denver's projects where she moved after the eviction, shades pulled, windows and door closed tight against any intrusion from the world, and strained for all she was worth to envision the seemingly unimaginable, the incongruous, the mildly strange to the certifiably bizarre.

15

She tried once for an hour before she fell asleep, exhausted. She didn't even move, except to turn over, until four in the afternoon. But usually her energy and her will gave out after only twenty minutes or so and she turned on the TV. The numbing stupidity of daytime programming was somehow comforting. She intuited that TV itself was proof she was far from alone in her lack of imagination. At least in America, she suspected, most people could envision nothing beyond their current circumstance, and television served as a diminished surrogate. Vicariously, at the very moment she stared at the tube, millions were fucking the same beautiful soap opera man/boy, projecting their fat and sweaty selves into the same perfect female form and humping ecstatically while the kids yowled and the bills dropped through the mail slot and the linoleum turned yellow.

Her failed exercises had seemed final proof Danny was right about her lack of imagination, but this was proof beyond any doubt whatsoever: a big man named Seth sat across a dingy desk from her. He was chewing on the end of what was left of his extinguished cigar and sweating like Cindy had never witnessed before. Lovers, boxers, and basketball players did not perspire in the heat of their respective games like this man did just sitting. Sweat ran from every inch of his substantial body. It was like Seth had to be this big to accommodate all his pores.

She was beginning to get used to the smell. It reminded her vaguely of her grandmother's farm on the eastern plains of Colorado, shit and sweat and the hired man's chewing tobacco when he stood too close after she got breakfast, trying to look down her shirt. But she could not take her eyes off Seth's nose. She feared it would explode it was so puffy, so reddish and blue like the skin was stretched too tight.

Seth had asked her to sound aroused. He wanted her to talk in a breathy voice and deeper than her natural one, to gurgle and coo and moan like she was about to explode, into flaming orgasm.

16

But she couldn't do it, no matter how badly she needed the job at Seth's phone sex service. She had seen the ad in the paper that morning and thought it sounded easy. "Talk to the lonely and make money," it said. The company was named Call Girls.

"Inevitably," Cindy thought as she read the paper on the couch, still naked after her ritual failed imagination exercise.

Now that she was here all she could do was look from Seth's nose, protruding like a misshapen erection just under his puffy eyes, to the script he'd given her and back at his nose. She intoned the words like she was giving the farm report on the radio: Oh Baby. Yeah, I want yours. All of it. How much ya got, Baby?

She might as well have said, "Hog futures down, soybeans $2.97 a bushel, wheat prices up slightly." Seth had suggested she imagine herself naked with the partner she liked best. He even got graphic with his description, which made Cindy nervous. Hung like a giraffe, he said. She thought for a moment that his description was for Seth's own lascivious pleasure, that he was planting seeds in her imagination but also his own, that maybe Seth was some strange voyeur of the mind. After all, what possesses a man to start such a business? Money alone? And how could there possibly be a woman anywhere who could get past that nose and those innumerable pores to keep his member tweaked?

But Seth's expression never changed. He glared at her. There was frustration in those deep set eyes to be certain, but not a hint of carnal energy that Cindy could see. A big blue vein in his nose began to throb.

"Well," he said, after a full five minutes of silence, "you gonna stare at me all day or you gonna talk dirty?"

His expression had not changed at all in the long minutes since his suggested scenario, as traffic passed outside on Colfax, the noise through the window distracting Cindy, as the phone rang a hundred times in the outer office without anyone ever answering it. Seth did chew his unlit cigar more vigorously, however.

17

Cindy tried to ignore the noise and leaned hard into memory. Danny had definitely been the best lover she ever had. He was passionate as a dog, but attentive to her needs, or so she interpreted his concern for their mutual pleasure, their mutual release. Most men were selfish in the sack. Their joy was all that mattered, and once that was achieved they went to sleep. She used to call Danny Superman for his effort to hold his own orgasm until she achieved hers, so they could arrive together, as he put it.

But she wholeheartedly hated Danny after finding a waitress dressed only in fishnet stockings in her bathroom one Friday afternoon. The only picture she could conjure of Danny in her imagination now was his head on a stick like a Popsicle, his tongue lolling, X's over his eyes like in a cartoon.

Cindy tried to imagine her first partner, a boy named Greg from high school who had reminded her of Clint Eastwood from his spaghetti western days. He had the same hard eyes and taut jaw, but she could only conjure those parts of him and not his naked body.

"How strange," she said out loud. They had talked about marriage briefly but broke it off when he announced he was going to join the Navy after graduation. She had cried a lot. Her virginity had sailed away on a tide of jism and sweat; an exchange of rings, a house, and kids were supposed to follow. They didn't and it hurt. She thought she was certainly a slut, maybe only a future slut, doomed to slutdom anyway, and it was his fault. Now she couldn't even see the boy in her mind.

Cindy's mother had told her at the time that she hadn't tried hard enough to keep Greg. "You should have forgotten to take a few pills," she had said.

A few years after graduation her mother sent her the hometown obituary page with a picture of Greg in his dress whites. He died of a drug overdose after two tours of Vietnam. There was a terse note in her mother's spidery handwriting: "So sad. Maybe if you'd married him."

18

"Well?" said Seth again. His eyes were beginning to glaze over and his dead cigar to droop.

Cindy tried harder to focus her concentration. Then there was Tony who worked with her at the doughnut shop her senior year, a fat Italian boy with chipped teeth and effete manners. But there was nothing to remember. One awkward bounce in his basement apartment after too much wine.

Then there was her boss at the shoe store after high school. Jimmy? Jerry, maybe? She couldn't remember.

Seth drummed his fingers on the desk and stared into space.

Then Bobby and Doc and John. All stupid men she had stupid conversations with about baseball and literature in bars, and slept with because she thought they were the three wise men, what with their many degrees and high flown language. It turned out they were the three stooges, all fingers in the eyes and bops on the chin. Her eyes. Her chin. Nothing good in the sex department to remember there.

In fact, the last time she saw Bobby and Doc and John she had summoned them to a bar not far from the campus where all three taught. It was filled with other academics and graduate students who longed to be academics, and she had stood on the bar and addressed them all. To the three stooges' shock and dismay she related all their short comings (all puns intended) to the crowd: Bobby's dick is about the size of a fuzzy caterpillar, Doc can't get it up unless reading Tolstoy, and John cries like a baby when he comes.

Seth began to hum absently, a bad version of the same song from Fiddler on the Roof Danny sang in the shower, If I were a rich man...deadle, deadle, deadle, deadle, deadle, deadle, deadle, dum...something like that.

Cindy searched in her memory frantically. Six months after she was divorced from Danny, she married Zig. He was an aging hippie ten years her senior who looked like Michelangelo's Poseidon. His graying hair was long and curly and thick, as was his

19

beard, in fact all the hair all over his body. They'd only had sex together once, just before the right reverend Blue Arrow, a white guy from Toronto who claimed to have been adopted by the Cree and who had a mail order minister's license, pronounced them man and wife. The sex may have been miraculous, but there were so many intoxicants of all varieties beforehand Cindy only vaguely remembered they had sex.

Zig departed immediately after the ceremony for Mexicali. He intended to invest his money in several kilos of pot, return home and sell them for enough profit to make a down payment on a love nest in one of Denver's lower-middle class suburbs. He waxed rhapsodic about late 50's era tract housing, kissed her, then got on his Harley and headed south.

He was arrested in Mexico two days later after making a buy from an undercover DEA agent and sentenced to 30 years of hard labor. Cindy had seen a write-up on it in the Denver Post two weeks after Zig left or she would have thought he merely found something else to do. According to the paper, the local drug enforcement people were very impressed with Mexico's judicial system, both its speed and its power. The paper informed her also, parole was not a concept the keepers of Mexican jails subscribe to.

Cindy had the marriage annulled the following day. She might lack imagination, she told her mother, but she was practical.

"Young lady, I am a busy man. Please send the next one in," said Seth as he checked her name off a list with a #2 pencil and yawned from the side of his mouth without the cigar in it.

The pencil had pictures of Spiderman swinging up and down its slender length. Cindy noticed that the threads he swung from disappeared into thin air.

"Subtraction," she said, more to herself than to Seth, who pretended not to hear.

"Another nut," he said as the door closed behind her.

Chapter 4

Zeke knew he wasn't smart. His mother told him when he was young. "You ain't no Einstein," she'd say. She said it when he broke the neighbor's window playing stick ball, when he fell off the front stoop and sprained his ankle while wrestling with Uncle Earl, when the retarded woman up the hall announced to the street when he was fourteen he was "boinking her," when he married Marianne.

His mother didn't like his choice in a wife at first. "She's so small. No kid's gonna slide from those skinny hips," she said and shook her head with disdain.

But she grew to love Marianne when she heard her whistle. "Such talent," she said then, and smiled and kissed her.

And his mother said "it" just now: "You ain't no Einstein." He'd called to tell her he was divorcing Marianne.

He said, "Yes, Ma. I ain't no Einstein."

Marianne had taken to saying "it" to him too the second year they were married. When he bounced a check. When he got a parking ticket. When he burned toast.

Now that he was getting rid of her, he'd have to start saying "it" to himself.

"No, Ma. You're just gonna have to believe I got my reasons. No. No. I'm not saying you need to mind your own business. Yes, I know she deserves better than me. Now she can go get better. Bye, Ma."

He hung the pay phone up with his mother in mid-sentence, "You ain't..." Click.

No, that he was not smart was a plain and simple fact he had accepted years before. He loved to read, but he didn't understand most of it. He just loved the sounds of words, the way words made pictures in his brain. School had been hard. College was out of the question. Being a clerk in the midst of books was the best he could possibly hope for. It was all he had ever wanted to do.

And he read there endlessly. The store where he worked was a small place catering mostly to the decadent readers of Denver's downtown. There were larger sections of Kerouac and the other beats, some South American poetry, leftist political tracts, Zen Buddhist meditation manuals, and the like. But there were also rarer things: books on Chinese painting techniques, on massage, herbal medicine, small press collections of anarchist poetry. It was like a proverbial candy store to a proverbial child, and, since he was the night clerk and customers dwindled to a rare few by early evening when downtown was given over to junkies, dealers, hookers and perverts, he could indulge himself much.

Zeke knew he was not smart, but that he had some power to foretell events before they actually occurred was becoming too clear to deny. Judy's death exactly as he had witnessed it in his mind, in dream and waking vision, was beginning to look like final proof that his strange visions did make him special among men, as Judy said, though he held that assertion open to debate, but that it was a gift from God as she also asserted seemed all the more absurd.

How could something so fallible and unutterably incomplete and terrifying and dizzying be a divine gift? It was more like a wedding gift from some perverse wizard who just happens to be a relation. Bourgeois politeness, that the lower classes mimic so energetically, dictates that it be acknowledged, maybe, but there's no warranty and you can't get rid of it. Like the 200 lb. wrought iron door-stop in the likeness of a giraffe with arthritic knees Marianne's grandmother had given them, or the monographed towel set that was a replica of the Shroud of Turin his mother sent last Christmas-a big Jesus corpse on the bath towel, smaller one on the hand towel, little bitty one on the washcloth. The Shroud as done by Warhol.

Sometimes the view of the future was clear, like Uncle Earl and Judy, but other times the messages were maddeningly cryptic. Before he was fired from his previous job as a forklift driver in an auto parts warehouse, he had seen his boss in a dream putting sticky notes all over his forehead. He intuited some sexual energy in the man's act and it made him nervous, even in his sleep, but he didn't have a clue that he'd get a pink slip that was really a sticky note. Get fucking lost, it said. You're fired.

For two weeks now he'd had a similarly convoluted dream. He saw Marianne everywhere dressed only in a white veil: in the bookstore, at home, at the bus stop, in the church where Judy's funeral was held. Sometimes she was holding hands with a man only vaguely familiar to him.

Only today had he deduced the meaning of this dream. Marianne was going to dump him for someone else. If she was going to be married he could only assume she must get rid of him soon, and he intended to beat her to the punch.

He had told Marianne he was going to a book signing at a big bookstore across town and wouldn't be home until after work. He then filed for divorce and called his mother. His plan was to let Marianne be served with the papers before he said anything, but now he felt guilty.

"She wasn't much of a wife," he thought, "but then he wasn't much of a husband, and they had been together for a while, and there may have been something worthwhile between them in the beginning and I just can't remember what it was...." So the internal dialogue went, endlessly.

And so he went home to tell her. He had just enough time to take a bus there, give her the news, hold her for a few minutes if she needed it, though the dream indicated otherwise, and catch the next bus downtown for work.

The apartment door was locked. For a moment he cursed his own stupidity. Marianne must have gone to the store. It was, after all, her day off. She had Tuesdays and Thursdays for her

23

"weekend" on this shift cycle at the computer circuit factory where she'd worked for four years, and she always did the marketing on one of her days off.

He let himself in. The curtains were drawn and the lights off, but he heard Marianne whistling a cantata in the bedroom.

Zeke took two steps before waves of déjà vu energy washed over him. The sensation was so strong he nearly fell down. He steadied himself against the dining room table and took deep breaths until his head cleared.

He heard a bass voice say, "Damn. You do that real good," as he stood before the closed door to the bedroom.

As when Judy died, he was not completely surprised, the sensations of despair and rage even felt somewhat familiar, but their depth and breadth was astounding. His stomach rumbled and his fists clenched. He raised his right foot to waist level and planted his foot just below the door knob. The door exploded off its hinges and landed on the foot of the bed.

He switched on the light to find Marianne sitting up in the bed with the blankets pulled up over her little breasts, as if he were a stranger to the room and her scrawny body. A big man was already scrambling for his clothes. Zeke recognized him as an unemployed plumber Marianne had met at night school and introduced to him once when he picked her up after class. He remembered how school girlish she looked as he pulled to the curb, with her books held to her chest and that goofy little smile.

The plumber was holding a tee shirt over his genitals with the words "This Marriage is Interrupted for the Football Season" on it. His huge hairy belly poked out over his hands. He smiled somewhat sheepishly, like he was embarrassed, but somehow also with arrogance.

"No offense, man," he said as he fumbled for his pants with one hand and held the tee shirt with the other. "I'll just get on outa here."

Marianne's eyes were big but she was otherwise expressionless. "The door," she said. "You've destroyed the door."

Zeke was calm now. The anger that had blown the door down smoldered in his chest. He felt like God, strong and beautiful and righteous, but he also felt empty, as hollow as a bell, and there was something far darker in him that he could not identify but that sent a small tremor of fear through his cerebral cortex. It originated in the deepest recesses of his brain and floated to the surface as a shudder, but sensed that it was vast and horrible.

He walked to the night stand on the opposite side of the bed from where the plumber struggled to pull his underwear from inside his pants, where they had somehow become entangled in his belt, without letting go of the tee shirt.

Nearly in a trance he took the revolver from the night stand drawer, a .32 Marianne insisted they keep for protection and that had warned would not stop a mildly intent dog.

Without a word he shot them both once between the eyes. Bang and bang. A flash of lightning, brief and irrevocable, then another.

Marianne slumped back against her pillow and the headboard immediately, the blanket falling from her small breasts. There was a perfect dark hole in her forehead. Her eyes were crossed. She looked like Raggedy Anne's twin, just like the big redheaded doll she'd propped against her pillow when she made the bed when they were first married.

The plumber tried to protest just as the bolt of lightning struck him square in the forehead. He stumbled backward a few steps with one hand raised, then forward. His eyes rolled upward as if they were trying to see the third eye had transplanted between them, then he dropped his shirt and sprawled across the bed, his face in Marianne's lifeless crotch.

"Would you behold her topped?" Zeke said out loud as he dropped the pistol at his feet, as his own eyes momentarily glazed over. He felt like weeping, but it passed.

25

"Look on the tragic loading of this bed..., the object poisons sight," said Zeke in the heightened diction of bad summer stock, and he left.

Only later, when he recounted the scene to Cindy, did he remember that the room smelled of Marianne and the plumber's sex, of room deodorizer meant to imitate roses but that did so only crudely, smelled like popcorn smothered in burned butter, which was one of Marianne's specialties.

Chapter 5

At an age when other young girls dreamt of being the subject of insipid love poems, Cindy dreamt her life would be great epic poetry: events and actions and emotions congealed to image and rhymed couplet. But by the time she took a night literature class at a community college in a Denver suburb shortly after she and Danny were married, it was obvious that could never happen.

"There are no more heroes," the professor had declared in a grandiose fashion, one arm raised in the air and his chin tilted toward the obscene incandescent lights. It seemed like a truism to her by then, hardly worthy of recognition, let alone ham posturing.

She certainly wasn't one. She hadn't yet arrived at her own declaration of life as a math operation, but she was clearly getting clues that loss was life's overarching theme.

She'd also never had a hero. In fact, she'd never met anyone else's either, or even heard a rumor of someone who might plausibly be one someday. If heroism existed at all, she had decided, it was not born of some inherent strength. It was not some sleeping seed that blossomed as its carrier aged, but action born of necessity, like one's own survival. Human selflessness, magnanimous self-sacrifice for others, or for some higher ideal, was a magnificent pan-species delusion.

Her father told her when she was a little girl that the old W.W.II veteran who begged for change in front of the Woolworth's every day, dressed in his uniform with all his medals like pressed flowers gleaming and his one pant leg neatly safety pinned, was a "true American hero." She believed that too until the old man tried to reach up her dress as she passed too close to his wheelchair when she was fourteen.

When he was found frozen stiff on her sixteenth birthday, her father, who knew nothing of the dress incident, cried great patriotic tears for "the old man's sacrifice."

Sacrifice made sense to her. The word meant something different for her, however, than for her father. The old man was a lamb of politics. He'd given up a part of himself, probably many parts the world couldn't see but that were just as pulverized as his leg, for some abstraction. In the end only a few remembered what he had done, what he'd lost, beyond the clichés: honor and freedom and duty, etc., etc.

She thought of the old soldier in night school, not when the class discussed Oedipus, but Eliot. He was far more Fisher King than tragic or vengeful warrior. Rather than get pissed and rave against the usurpers of his dignity, all those brain-dead passersby who dropped coins into his tin cup and mouthed patriotic pieties, he had gone as equally dead behind the eyes, more so perhaps for what he had seen, maybe what he had done. Cindy imagined his leg buried somewhere at the edge of the wasteland, a ritual sacrifice from which nothing could grow for the sterility of the soil.

She was in the wasteland now. This was no battlefield, per se, but nearly as dead, as decadent. The shadows of the buildings along Colfax were merging as the February sun descended toward the mountains.

The street she walked, where Seth's office was located, was home to whores and drug dealers. It was also near the downtown business district. At this time of day the guard changed, so to speak. Men and women in tailored suits and carrying briefcases, with a faraway look in their eyes, were replaced by men in denim and black leather and women in tight short skirts and fake fur, most with the same faraway look in their eyes.

"Two sides of the same economic coin," thought Cindy.

She had wanted to catch a bus immediately after she left Call Girls, but the system was between shifts. All the buses were headed out of the metro area carrying commuters toward the suburbs and the illusion of home and wouldn't be back for another hour or so, for the second wave of outbound and to resume the nightly runs from the projects to downtown and back. The second shift.

She had needed air anyway, however dank with exhaust and general debauchery, after her "interview." Cindy had not only taken her failure of imagination to heart, but the future had grown bleaker with her failure to get the job. "Not to mention," she thought, "as far as love goes, hell as far as sex goes, I'm a multiple car pile-up on the freeway of life. Mom was more than right about my prospects after Greg. Bleak, she told me. Should be my damned name. Probably will be my damned epitaph after I starve to death in the near future, unhoused and insufficiently laid, not to mention loved."

She turned the collar of her winter coat up, even though it was warm for a February at the foot of the Rockies. The day's events had drained the blood from her. She walked the street, up and down both sides, for hours, long after the buses returned. Pictures of exploding noses, rosettes of blood big as carnations and some unidentified viscous substance the color of urine, were all she could conjure to her mind.

28

Chapter 6

What brings a man to this, Zeke thought: to the murder of a wife he did not love, the daughter of a woman he might have loved, the murder of his wife's lover whom he neither knew nor hated? What brings a man here without any pangs of guilt whatsoever, his only act of remorse the asking of this very question, the need to know why he feels no remorse? (Though of course there is a kind of remorse born of his fear of the American judicial and penal systems.) What brings a man to hungering for his own death, in spite of his moral and emotional shortcomings?

"How can a man feel such unequivocal despair if he, seemingly, has no conscience at all, only a limited capacity for love, and no intelligence?" he asked aloud.

His head was beginning to hurt. "I ain't no Einstein," he said and was certain the pain was the result of an ethical dilemma beyond his capacity to solve. He wished Judy were still alive to ask. Such things were right up her alley, but he was her daughter's killer now. What could she possibly have to say to him?

The floor above him began to thump wildly at the same time the wall next to the bed on which he lay began to thump even more wildly. A deep male groan came through the ceiling.

"Another night at the Fuckfest Inn," Zeke wanted to shout, but didn't.

The primal rhythms coming from the plaster had been the same every night for the last three weeks. He had been at a loss as to what to do after he shot Marianne and her lover, so he went to work. He reread Othello, which was the only work he could think of at the time that encompassed circumstances that resembled his own.

He walked around the shop the rest of the night saying, in his best bad English actor's voice, "Would you behold her topped?" An endless vision hung in the air before him of the fat plumber on top of Marianne: his huge white ass going up and down like a piston, her skinny legs sticking out from under him like a mechanic under a car that is on a hydraulic jack gone mad.

He paced through the entire night at the bookstore, trying to decide what to do, though he locked up as usual at 11:00. He knew he couldn't fall on some proverbial sword like a tragic hero. He neither had the courage or incentive, like love or honor. Besides, his story had already gone contrary to Shakespeare's. Othello had taken rumor for surety and actually loved the woman he killed, or so he said. Zeke wasn't even sure he liked Marianne, her mindless and simpering ways. He might not be Einstein, but then neither was she. He'd also taken surety for surety. He had definitive, ocular proof.

"And there was no Iago," Zeke said aloud at one point. "Unless I am both Iago and Othello, some schizo villain within a hero, or vice versa."

His head had hurt, and he had wished Judy were still alive, and he had asked for the first time, "But what could she possibly have to say to me now?" in mid-stride before a display of pop-psychology books by a guy with an Indian name. He also knew he could not confess and go to jail. He watched his Uncle Earl melt there. Earl's eyes went gray and lightless and his shoulders rolled forward toward the ground before he was forty. It was a cliché, but Earl was nothing but a shell, an empty husk, when Zeke saw him last; and that was a long time ago and Earl was still there.

He also knew he couldn't beat the system. All evidence pointed to him, and he didn't have enough money to hire a lawyer smart enough and connected enough, or forensics people with their own data to refute the state's data, or private investigators to discredit the witnesses who inevitably saw him on his way home and heard the shots and saw him leave.

30

So in the morning he emptied the till in lieu of the paycheck he would have gotten that day (plus some), walked to his bank and withdrew the money in the checking and Christmas club accounts, walked two blocks up 14th from where Cindy now pictures the messy demise of Seth's nose, and checked into this run-down wino hotel.

His boss at the bookstore told him once that Neil Cassidy's old man died in this hotel. Someone certainly had. The whole place, dimly lit hallways, the lobby, his room, smelled of death, and rancid urine.

Zeke had spent every day of the last three weeks in his room, a seven-dollar-a-day-ten-foot-by-ten-foot cell with a toilet and sink in one corner. He dared only go out at night, and then only briefly to get the meager supplies he lived on, mostly Wonder bread and bologna, and even in the dark he went as incognito as possible. He wore a trench coat he'd taken from the bookstore, left there by a customer nearly a year before, some wrap-around sunglasses he'd purchased at a nearby Mini Mart and that made night three times darker for him, and a Cubs hat he stole from a young man passed out on a bus stop bench.

He fit right in with the rest of the nighttime-downtown-population, though the quality of the coat and the cleanliness of the cap made him look more like one of the suburban guys who showed up on Friday and Saturday nights looking to pay for sex, or looking for a life in so unlikely a place, than like one of the regulars.

He told himself the same joke he'd told himself for three weeks, each night when the walls began to shake:

Home is where the women come and go and have never heard of Michelangelo, where they come, and then come, and go, only to come again, to come and go.

31

The joke was funny as hell the first time. T. S. Eliot was surely rolling in his grave, a thought that made Zeke inexplicably happy. But it wasn't funny thereafter. It was more a ritual, just something to say everyday at the same time, like Uncle Earl had always said, "See ya in the funny papers," at the end of his visits to Attica. He'd gone once a month, every second Sunday, for three years before he moved from New York City for good. See ya in the funny papers. Indeed.

Zeke's head throbbed. He had watched a spider spin a web in the corner of the room for hours, the most entertainment he'd had in weeks, since the thrill of visualizing the acts that produced the mad thumping wore off, then fell asleep and dreamt of webs. The entire city was covered with sticky silk thread, beautiful and treacherous. It hung from every skyscraper, every car, every wino. It hung from stop lights and hookers' tits and bandannaed street warriors, from the few trees downtown, from buses and fire hydrants. It hung from everything but Zeke.

At the end of his dream he had grabbed a single filament, big as a rope, that seemed to hang from the stars. He swung from it, out over the broken buildings, and headed south. He flew like an awkward bird high above the cars on I-25 between the Denver skyline and the Front Range; but toward what destination?

The speed of the flight had turned his stomach upside down and inside out. He woke up with the same ringing in his ears, the same disequilibrium as came with his waking visions, the same nausea and dizziness that had ridden on the back of this dream three days straight now.

He had to leave his room for a while. He needed air and aspirin, and he had a sudden craving for orange juice.

32

Chapter 7

There had been a rack of magazines next to Judy's toilet, mostly *Time* and *Good Housekeeping*. Zeke didn't understand. "Who the hell wants to sit in his own vapor long enough to read anything?" he had asked Marianne after their first visit to her mother's house.

He had, however, taken up the habit of sitting on the pot for a couple of hours at a time in his new abode at the Regency Arms, wino and nookie hotel. It gave him his only change of perspective. He could stare at the bed from the toilet rather than staring at the toilet from the bed. It was a simple inversion, but the only alternate view he had available, since the room was small and the only window was about twelve inches from the brick building next door.

Zeke used the toilet before he put on his "disguise," but only briefly. He had to get out of the room as quickly as possible. His nerves tingled and his ears roared. He was beginning to see spider webs everywhere without being asleep.

The cool air, though warm for February in Colorado, cleared his head a little. After the continual smell of years' worth of piss, even the acrid odor of big city industrial waste that wafted over the street was a relief.

Zeke headed for the small grocery on Colfax. He had tended, so far, not to walk on any streets but the side ones that crossed Colfax, because of the human activity on that decadent thoroughfare and the subsequent police presence; but tonight he needed a change of routine, any change however small, albeit incongruously dangerous as well.

He had been afraid of those darker walks down the side streets his first few nights out, and for good reason. At the beginning of his second week at the hotel he passed several Hispanic youths in black jackets and bandannas lounging against a dumpster. They followed him, then surrounded him. Several knives were brandished and they requested his money.

Zeke's adrenaline had raged beyond the bounds of anything he had ever experienced. All he could see was himself in prison. He had already begun to wish for his own death, but what if he didn't die and the cops came and took him to a hospital to plug his holes and his identity was discovered?

He grabbed the nearest young man, in wrap-arounds just like his own and sporting a little mustache, by the lapels of his leather coat and began to spin.

He hit several of the gang members in the circle around him with the young man's feet as both Zeke and his "weapon" screamed like they were on the roller coaster at Lakeside. Then Zeke threw him into the street, bouncing him off the roof of a passing car, and growled spontaneously like a bad dog. All he could hear were the sounds of running feet on the sidewalk as he struggled to regain his composure.

Since then no one had bothered him. He had passed several young men in black leather on his trips out for groceries and the bad mystery novels grocery stores sell, some Hispanic, some white, some black. They always stopped talking as he passed, and watched him from the corners of their collective eyes.

He'd seen the young man with the mustache a couple of times. "*Que pasa*, Loco Man?" he said. Zeke had offered a low guttural growl in response, just to keep their relationship well defined.

Tonight he walked straight for Colfax, then turned left into the neon-saturated strangeness of the street. A sign on the other side blinked on and off: "Tits, Tits, Tits," it said.

Loud music washed out of a bar on Zeke's side of the street, and he was tempted to go in. Bars had always depressed him, let alone bars where women pushed their pretty little muffs into cold chrome bars and swung their breasts in time to heavy metal music.

Earl had taken him to such places on the Jersey shore when he was only seventeen, during Earl's brief stay outside Attica. Zeke had gotten an erection and cried for all the decadence the first time. Uncle Earl had laughed his way to tears.

"You're a poet, boy," he'd said. "You want to fuck 'em and save 'em. Typical poet's confusion. Us regular guys just want to bang one of these fine young things till our whackers fall off."

Earl had picked up two of the dancers that first night and they all drove to a beach covered with litter when the topless place closed. Zeke could hear Earl and one of the women laughing ecstatically from the car as he and the other one walked on the sand holding hands. She was young, barely eighteen, with soft green eyes and reddish curls. They had kissed good night in the back seat of Earl's Ford.

He found out later Earl had paid the women a hundred dollars. Zeke had wept again. His first broken heart.

He passed by the bar, pushing his way through the music as it rolled out the door, and he did not look up when two women in spike heels and skirts the size of wash cloths made sucking noises with their lips at him.

He was lonely, and horny from listening to the hookers and their customers for weeks, but the risk would be too great. Besides, he had no idea what he would do when his money ran out, as it would in only a few more weeks if all he did was stay at the hotel and eat bologna.

The young Pakistani man was behind the counter at the grocery as usual. Zeke had figured out early on that the only English he knew were the names of the store's products. He seemed to have memorized them all and their exact location.

"Aspirins generic and Bayer, aisle 2," he said to Zeke's query. "Orange juice, in your grocer's refrigerator section." The poor bastard had obviously learned some of his English from TV, Zeke thought. He probably thinks we all talk in incomplete sentences and trademarked clichés.

35

He had asked the location of the items so as to spend as little time as possible in the brightly lit store. Now he was regretting being here at all. A pretty red haired woman, auburn to strawberry blonde actually, like Judy, Zeke thought, was staring at him over a Spiderman comic book.

He figured his photograph, probably from his driver's license, and probably pictures of the sheet draped corpses, would be on all three Denver network stations. They'd probably interrupted programming right after the bodies were found to run the pictures the first time.

It wasn't that the Denver news people were incredibly civic minded, or that double murders were rare here, but the competition among the three affiliates was fierce. It had made their coverage of such events at least as tawdry as it was depressing.

He hadn't seen a television in weeks, but he figured even the Denver TV people's attention had probably been redirected by now, hopefully some time ago. After all, none of the participants was famous and he had not mutilated the bodies. It took either fame or extreme mayhem to hold the public's attention.

Maybe the woman who stared at him from beside the rack of comic books was merely more attentive than most viewers. God, maybe she's a cop, he thought and he choked back the bile that rose in his throat.

As nonchalantly as he could Zeke carried his items to the counter. The woman waited behind him to pay for a stack of comics, and Zeke did his best to keep his face turned as far from her as possible, though she seemed to be moving slightly to his left, then to his right. He thought he caught a glimpse of her in his peripheral view.

"She's trying to get a better look," he thought, and turned his head a few degrees, first left and then right, to match her movements.

"Everyone on the floor!" someone shouted.

It's over, Zeke thought, and his heart broke. For himself, for Marianne, for Judy, for Uncle Earl. He swallowed hard as he got to the floor, as tears rose to his eyes behind his sunglasses.

"Anybody moves and I'll blow their fuckin' head off," another voice boomed.

Zeke could see feet move by him and disappear around the counter. He could also see the redhead lying not too far from him. He thought at first she was praying. She had her hands to her mouth, but her eyes were on the guy with the gun. If there was any fear there, Zeke could not detect it. She looked either resigned or curious. Zeke could not decide which.

"Open the safe," the first voice hollered.

There was more cursing when the clerk answered in a stream of syllables only a few people within many thousands of miles would have understood, then a shotgun blast. The feet ran past going the other way.

The redhead got up and moved stealthily behind the counter. Zeke stood in time to see her retching. The poor Pakistani man was on the floor, behind the register with its empty drawer hanging out like a tongue, sans his head. Tears flowed from Zeke like they hadn't since he was a child, like they hadn't for Judy or Marianne and the plumber. The clerk's smile, that Zeke just realized was the reason he came here instead of going to the Mini Mart that was closer to the hotel, a small beacon in this wasteland, was as big as the cosmos now.

Zeke headed for the door.

"Wait a minute," the redhead said, wiping her mouth on her sleeve. "The cops will want to ask you questions."

"All I saw were feet," Zeke said over his shoulder as he walked out into the neon night thick with sirens.

Chapter 8

Altruism is the most completely human quality, Zeke thought, and the most antithetical to survival.

Altruism is dead, thought Cindy.

She had followed Zeke from the store after only a moment's hesitation. Of course he was right. All she'd seen were feet too. All she'd heard were shouts in male voices. But she'd have to make a statement, look at mug shot books, anyway. Do they have photos of feet and recordings of voices, she thought? *Ridiculous.*

The man in the trench coat was already across the street and headed away from the lights of the bars and porn shops toward the utter blackness beyond when she stepped outside.

"Hey!" she shouted.

He turned his head only slightly and kept walking. She followed just as the light turned against her and was nearly hit by a pink Cadillac, all its windows darkened, the rear one in the shape of a heart.

"Probably an omen," she thought as the car squealed away and police cars roared upon all sides of the store, but she followed the man in the trench coat and Cubs hat anyway.

She could see him walking away from her, faster now, when her eyes adjusted to the lower level of light. She started to walk faster. He started to trot. She took off her heels and ran too. He was at a full gallop after two blocks. He turned the corner.

"You bastard!" she yelled with the last of her breath when she reached the corner where he'd turned. She couldn't see his silhouette at all.

Cindy leaned against the building breathing heavily. "You'd leave me here to get raped, or worse," she said to herself.

"Altruism is definitely dead. Hell, we're past rigor mortis and the worms are nearly done with their banquet on altruism's silly heart."

"What do you want?" said a voice from the dark doorway twenty feet from Cindy.

Her heart nearly jumped out of her chest, one great ka-thump, and she was more alert than ever in her life.

"Tell me you're the guy in the Cubs hat and sunglasses," she said. She held a shoe in each hand like a weapon. "And if you're not or even if you are and you try to touch me I'll scream for all I'm worth and run for the cops at that grocery up there where there's just been a murder and I'll tell 'em you did it." She took a breath. "Motherfucker," she said as an afterthought, trying to sound tough, or at least like she meant what she said.

Zeke stepped out of the doorway. Cindy could make out his outline against the streetlight that glowed anemically a block behind him.

He repeated, "What do you want?"

Cindy raised the shoe in her right hand over her head. It was obvious she was not armed, but she still could be a cop. He hoped he could still outrun her if things didn't go well. But he wasn't sure.

"First, what are your intentions?" Cindy asked.

"To go home, such as it is," Zeke said. "Why are you following me?"

Cindy lowered her shoe. "Well, to tell the truth, at first I just thought you were kind of cute, what I can see of you. Then it dawned on me that you look familiar. I thought and thought, and then I realized...you, uh, look like the guy..."

Cindy blushed violently, though Zeke could not see it. Zeke figured she knew, that she remembered his face from TV.

"Go on," he said, expecting the indictment of recognition, to be called vile names like wife-killer, slayer-of-overweight-plumbers, Iago/Othello-schizoid-combination-platter, villain-without-a-clue.

"Well," Cindy stammered. "You look kinda like the guy who turns into Spiderman."

Chapter 9

Two weeks later, at Zeke's suggestion, Cindy purchased a 900 line and an extra phone, contracted with an agency to collect the money for her, and set up a phone sex service in her apartment. Cindy Sweet became Cindy Sweet Stuff, the phone sex queen, in her advertisements in both the Post and the News.

Zeke had insisted she talked dirty better than anyone he ever met after she recounted her ordeal with Seth, that any man would pay good money to hear her whisper nasty nothings.

"You're just partial, Reilly," she had said as she kissed her way down his belly.

"You're right," he said and shuddered under the electricity of her lips, his imagination mapping her road south to his primary erogenous zone. "I've certainly never had sex like we have, but then I've never cared about anybody this much."

Cindy kissed her way back up his belly, and over his right nipple. She laid her head upon his chest. He could see tears welling in her eyes.

"I have no imagination," she had told him that first night they met, in the cab ride to her apartment. A confession.

"And I ain't no Einstein," he had said. It was a reply, not merely a counter assertion, but a kind of melodic chorus that had melted all her common sense into a romantically concupiscent puddle. They kissed for the first time as the cabby watched in the rear view.

They'd made love for nearly three days from the time they met until Zeke's phone sex suggestion, but things hadn't started well.

Zeke hadn't wanted Cindy to go "home" with him and it miffed her. She thought he must be married. He explained what went on at the hotel, however, and she suggested they talk over coffee in a restaurant that was, coincidentally, next door to the bookstore, site of Zeke's former employment. He told Cindy there were circumstances he couldn't explain but that made public contact impossible. Now she was certain he was married and his suggestion they go to her apartment one more proof of male madness-for-pussy-at-all-costs brought on by excessive quantities of hormones raging in their hairy bodies.

She had told him so, at the top of her lungs. Several young men in black leather with earrings and dark glasses and pale blue bandannas walked up to investigate. Zeke growled and the men stepped lightly around them. "Que pasa, Loco Man," said one of the young men and tilted his head sharply upward in sign of greeting. Zeke growled again.

Cindy had been terrified: of the young gangbangers, of Zeke's primal behavior. But she also flushed with an excitement that bordered on the sexual.

Zeke had sat down on the curb. "My mother has told me since I was a kid," he began, "that no lie is a good lie. Bad advice in many, maybe even most circumstances, but her endless assertion has made me prone to a near Catholic guilt." Zeke was appalled at this turn of events: a killer who feels, at best, a modicum of remorse for his crime wracked with guilt over a lie to someone he does not know.

He spilled the whole story to Cindy. He even confessed his lust for his mother-in-law. Cindy had sat silently through the telling, had gone through every negative emotion she knew as if she were sampling which response felt correct. Fear. Repugnance. Simple disdain. Anger at his lack of remorse (which he also confessed). Sadness for the dead. She settled on a kind of depression, more for the folly of her species than anything else, she decided, though there was a decidedly empty feeling at her own

41

membership in that species; and the swirling morass of sheer and unadulterated folly that had been her so-called life thus far.

Cindy had wanted to cry, but didn't.

Zeke had wanted to cry too, a long, hard, cathartic wail, but he didn't either.

Chapter 10

Like their first conversation, their first night of lovemaking had not started out auspiciously either. They were half undressed before they got the door to Cindy's apartment open, and flung themselves on the couch without bothering to pull it out into a bed, or to remove the cat. Cindy was scratched multiply on one shoulder before Zeke could get off of her and she could get off of the cat.

To Cindy's surprise the pain only seemed to heighten her arousal. Even more to her surprise were the sounds that came out of her the first time Zeke entered her.

The only sound she ever made during sex in the past had been when Danny touched her clitoris just so once and it tickled. She had giggled, which so discomfited Danny he took a cold shower and didn't talk to her for three days.

With Zeke she moaned from the second he was inside her, and then so chaotically Zeke wasn't sure if this was joy or pain.

She made more noise even than the women in a porn movie he'd seen once at a stag party for his cousin Willie entitled, appropriately enough, The Screamers. The women in the movie hollered unto over-acting.

Zeke could detect no acting at all in Cindy's voice and he stopped three times to ask if she was OK Of course, Cindy said yes the first two times. The third time she slapped him on top of the head so hard his teeth clacked together. She told him if he didn't hump her forthwith she would do serious harm in his nether regions, that at the moment the muscles of her nether-realm could squash a truck.

During that first 30 minutes the range of Cindy's vocalizations astounded even her, especially her: from a contrite whisper, to growls like Zeke's growl at the gangbangers, to moans, to language she did not know she knew until it exited her lips. A small voice began to ask, what the hell is wrong with you, but was immediately squashed by a hundred ton, "OH-MY-GOD!" It was a traditional, even clichéd response to her own orgasm, but at least ten decibels higher than is safe for human ear drums.

Zeke's right ear rung even now, two weeks later and a thousand miles away. He didn't mind. The ringing served as a constant reminder of their all-too-brief 36 hours together.

Chapter 11

Cindy Sweet Stuff's Phone Sex Service received only two calls the first day of business, and neither caller seemed particularly impressed with Cindy's acumen. Even the guy Cindy assumed from his octave jumping voice still had pimples and would have to explain the charges to his mom.

"Geez," he said. "What a gyp."

The second day Cindy took five calls and experimented a little. She learned much about the interplay of male aberrational sex schemes that day and their ostensibly female impetus. Men don't really want the actual particulars, but an enhanced version, because masculine fantasies are, she realized, like the male view of the perfect woman as reflected in advertising—the product of a dream rather than anything real, except accidentally so. The women in the ads are mutants, a genetic oddity that happens to conform physically to the dream, to accidentally conform like every mutation is an accident. The only close male equivalent she could think of were the morphodites who play basketball.

What she needed, she further realized, was a ham actor's delivery and a script full of unusual metaphors. So after caller number four she wrote one, and when number five called she blew his socks off-no puns intended.

By day three Cindy Sweet Stuff was the best in the business. She played riffs like a jazz saxophonist, first bouncing off the caller's imagination, then heightening his fantasies like the best of harmony players, then blowing the top off the fantasy by taking over, creating the melody, leading the poor fool on the other end of the phone places he'd never been, never knew existed, leaving him limp and exhausted and probably deeply in debt to Cindy Sweet Stuff.

It wasn't long before Cindy was putting in ten hour days and decided to take on help. She ran the phone a few hours a day, then went out recruiting. A recorded message to make a grown man weep with desire kept the customers calling, anxiously hoping she had returned.

Cindy hired a black waitress named Zoe who served her coffee at the International House of Pancakes, an unemployed white woman on welfare right out of the welfare line, two hookers off Colfax after she saw their pimp slap one of them, a Korean woman in a tent-sized sarong after a guy on Geraldo told America that slurred r's and l's gave him an erection.

She trained them in her technique, paid them all in cash, even hired a nanny to keep the welfare mother's kids. Within a month she moved the whole operation to an office in a mini-mall just outside the metro area. She also put a substantial down payment on a condo a few blocks from the office.

She'd bought the first 900 line with the very last of her money. But now her income was unimaginable. That first day, when she got only two calls, she thought the world must be a far better place than she previously believed possible. The number of perverts in the world, however, proved to be beyond her most extreme estimate. Even after her generous payroll, all in cash, she took in thousands and thousands a month. She got a bank account, bought a Mercedes, set up college funds for her employees and their kids...and she got a lawyer.

At the end of their three day love-fest, when they finally returned to the world, Zeke and Cindy discovered that fate had not been altogether kind in bringing them together.

Cindy had made a batch of cookies from the recipe on the side of a cereal box, cinnamon apple snickerdoodles, to rejuvenate them after their prolonged exertions while Zeke lay on the couch watching cartoons. The recipe said it made five dozen, but Cindy made the cookies as big as pancakes and got two.

They were nearly through with the whole batch, with coffee since Zeke had left his orange juice on the floor of the grocery along with the generic aspirin and Cindy's pile of comics, when the news came on.

They both nearly choked on chunks of snickerdoodles at the sight of themselves at the store. There Zeke was in his disguise, and Cindy behind him, and the poor Pakistani clerk. The film stopped just as a hooded gunman's shotgun threw flames.

The newsman said the police were still looking for the gunmen, for an unidentified redheaded woman in her late thirties or early forties, and for Reilly, wife-killer and shooter-of-plumbers and cleaner-out-of-bookstore-tills.

Cindy had suggested a lawyer at the time, but Zeke had declined. Lawyers cost money he did not have and a public defender would, at best, get him only a year or two less than no lawyer at all. He dressed and was headed for the edge of town, in a ski jacket that had belonged to Danny and a Colorado Rockies hat of Cindy's, within ten minutes.

Now, if Zeke ever returned so she could talk him into it, or was captured, she had money enough to hire the best. And, in fact, according to a recent poll of defense attorneys the best criminal lawyer among their ranks, right up there with Racehorse Haines and some guy from Wyoming who dressed like Gene Autry, was a member of one of Denver's largest law firms, one Johnny Quarrels.

So she had called him. She gave no details but said she had a boyfriend who might be needing his expert services. She sent him a ten-grand retainer in cash via her very large Korean employee, and Johnny Quarrels sent her a receipt and a request they talk in greater detail at her earliest convenience.

Dear Ms. Sweet Stuff, it had said.

"Nicest thing a man has called me in months," thought Cindy, and nearly got tearful thinking of.

Interlude

Roses, sex, popcorn, and scorched butter. At Judy's funeral, the smells had so occupied Zeke as somehow meaningful that he forgot something else his heightened senses had allowed him to witness.

To the left of the altar was a great golden cross that looked like some kind of medieval weapon, a halberd perhaps. A small tan spider hung from one arm of the cross, lowered itself as it spun its life line from its own body an inch at a time.

The spider descended to about 5 feet from the floor, then hung motionless for several minutes in the stagnant air of the church.

It had begun to throw out lines of web onto the air, as if it intended to build one on the void, when Zeke realized it was seeking a path, something to connect to.

Filament after filament lay on the air like a flag only to fall to the floor. Then one caught the collar of an altar boy, who looked bored with his task, and the spider clambered over the line. It threw another web from the boy's ear to the priest's hand where he held up the chalice and chanted, walked over to, then up, the priest's hand and sat on the lip of that ritual bowl.

46

Zeke was not sure, but he thought the spider drank there, a long, spider-sized draught of transubstantiated blood.

Part Two

I drifted on a river I could not control,
No longer guided by the bargeman's ropes.
They were captured by howling Indians
Who nailed them naked to colored stakes.
                    -Rimbaud, "The Drunken Boat"

Chapter 12

Zeke had cursed his luck all night long. The only night of his life he'd ever spent out of doors, and the previously unseasonable weather had to turn seasonable. The temperature dropped to around 20 degrees and a knife-like wind fell from the north. There were snowflakes in the air as the alley where he sat grew gray with first light.

After seeing himself on TV Zeke had headed west from Cindy's apartment. He knew the train tracks ran the length of Denver from north to south and he intended to catch a southbound freight. He had no idea where, specifically, he'd go and what he'd do when he got there, but catching a train out of town was all he could think of.

His new disguise was different from the pictures on television, but not much, and it was only a matter of time now until someone identified him. There was speculation in the local media, absurd as it was, that Zeke was involved in the grocery holdup somehow, and there was a reward for information leading to the capture of the clerk's killers put up by the store's owner. More for PR or as a warning to any future-would-be-robbers, Zeke speculated, than to revenge his underpaid clerk. But insipid assertions by the media and public relations tactics by heartless rich men aside, money would motivate the public to a new level of attentiveness. He had to get out of town.

The tracks proved to be further than he thought. He knew from the cabby's initial protestations the night he went home with Cindy that her apartment was on the edge of Five Points, but he only knew the place by its violent reputation. Its actual location was more a relative direction from downtown to him, and he and Cindy had been too preoccupied with each other to watch the cab's route.

He walked by row upon row of brick apartment buildings built for low income families decades ago. The cold front had settled in as the sun began to go down and very few people were about. A few cars went by, but mostly nothing moved. Then he walked by row upon row of much older brick warehouses, and finally came to the high chain link that signaled the railroad right-of-way.

A train was just squeaking to a halt as he scrambled over the fence in the dark. The first freight car door he pulled on opened. He climbed up into the doorway and waited for his eyes to adjust. Except for a broken crate and some straw in one corner the car was empty, but it smelled of human occupation like the Regency Arms: stale cigarette smoke and rancid piss.

Zeke squatted in the corner opposite the straw and broken crate, but then realized the urine smell was strongest there. He sat down on the straw and waited for the train to take him southward.

He waited and he waited. He stood and stamped his feet to get blood to them. He twisted side to side and beat his hands together. The train didn't move.

Just before midnight Zeke heard voices outside the car. He peeked around the edge of the open doorway and could make out two figures with flashlights moving toward him down the track. They stopped at every door and pushed it open and shined the beams of their lights into the cars.

Zeke's stone cold feet no more hit the ground than the men with the lights spotted him from three cars away. They shouted and gave chase. Zeke hoped railroad cops didn't carry guns. He hoped they weren't nearly as angry as they sounded.

He had a head start and the fence was not more than 200 yards, but he'd eaten nothing in three days but Cindy's snickerdoodles and most of his blood had rushed from his feet and legs, to keep his major organs warm in response to the severe weather. He felt like he was moving in slow motion. The railroad cops gained on him to the point that he reached the fence just ahead of them.

The sound of their footsteps on the gravel and their curses on the wind so close behind him engendered a vision of Earl behind bars and he leapt on the fence with a jolt of fear induced adrenaline. He grabbed the fence top with one hand, pulled himself up until he could reach over the fence and grab the chain link well down the opposite side with the other, then vaulted over like he'd seen kids do in schoolyards when he was young. He had been too afraid to try it then and stuck to using the gate.

Zeke ran into the dark like a sprinter as his pursuers yelled obscenities from the other side of the fence. He stopped running after several blocks and ducked down an alley between warehouses to escape the wind and any police cruisers.

He pulled his legs up under the ski jacket Cindy had given him and huddled against some concrete steps in a vain attempt to maintain his adrenaline and exertion induced warmth. He had fallen into an uneasy sleep only as the air turned gray with the first wash of light.

A voice jolted him awake now.

"Onanist! Damnable onanist," said the man on the steps above him. He was looking down at Zeke over a railing made of two inch pipe. Zeke could see the man's breath on the air.

He pulled his legs out of his coat and stretched them in front of him. His joints popped and the pain of moving his legs after so many hours made him groan.

"A man without a woman is an onanist, by definition," said the man, "an abomination before God, a dark spot on the luminous beauty of the creation, a sacrilege, an onerous creature hard for even the Son of Man to love."

His tone was officious, his diction heightened. There was a small southern tinge to his voice. He shook a great finger at Zeke as he spoke. Against his will, Zeke cowered momentarily under the man's finger and before his eyes that were harsh and dark under great eyebrows that grew together over them.

53

"What do you have to say for yourself, oh child of Onan?" said the man.

"Nothing," Zeke said. "I will leave as soon as the blood comes back into my feet."

The man grabbed the pipe rail and vaulted over it, over, to the ground.

"Rise!" he shouted, as Zeke trembled. "Walk, sinner!"

Zeke vigorously kneaded his legs with his hands and tried to stand. He had to hold the railing to stay up and never took his eyes off the man who stood next to him now, with his head bowed and his arms outstretched.

"The Lord works in mysterious ways," said the man. "The power of prayer is an ominous power."

He took Zeke's hand and shook it rapidly.

"For days I have prayed for your arrival and now here you are, just in the nick of time." His eyes had softened, and the man's delivery had softened too, though not completely.

"You must be hungry," he said. "Let's get you some sustenance. Then I'll introduce you to Cantarita." He took Zeke by the arm, who now realized he was weaker than he thought, and not just from cold and his fetal position, but for lack of food. Though still wary, he was in no position to refuse.

The man helped Zeke up the concrete steps, four in all. Zeke knew because with each one a pain shot from both ankles to both hips. The man looked up and down the alley then opened the steel door to the warehouse and helped Zeke through.

The air was warm and there was a flickering circle of light just ahead. As they got closer Zeke could see that a gas pipe had been pried away from the wall and taken apart at a joint and that the gas flowing out of the pipe had been lit, the source of both heat and light in the room. The flame was blue and about eighteen inches long. It made a small roaring sound.

Zeke's host sat him in the only chair to be seen and handed him a plate of cold beans, then another and a cup of coffee after he devoured the first plateful without taking a breath.

Chapter 13

Zeke slept for twenty-four hours straight, without a single dream, under a wool blanket on a mattress that smelled of mold. He woke up to the roar of the gas flame and the smell of coffee. The man who had led him here held a pot before the fire. Flames reached around either side.

"It is time to meet Cantarita," he said.

"Who, and why?" said.

"This is why you are here," said the man, "the answer to my prayer." Zeke was certain this was all the explanation he would get.

The man led Zeke through the warehouse, a great dark space that held nothing but dark. Must be where they keep all the darkness the human race can't use up immediately, Zeke thought, a darkness warehouse. He could hear their footsteps echo off the walls.

The man opened a door just like the one in the alley and they stepped into light. They were in another room, still large but smaller than the room with the flame at one end. What little daylight the overcast sky allowed shone through large windows several feet up the room's high walls.

A woman sat against the far wall reading. Zeke could see she was about his age, a few years younger perhaps, that she was Native American with high, smooth cheekbones and small epicanthic eye fold, that she read Rimbaud's Illuminations. Zeke had sold a copy to a teenager in a black beret with a gold ring in her nose his last night at the bookstore.

The woman looked up at the echo of their footsteps.

"Here he is," said the man. "I told you he would come. Prayer is very powerful," he said as he walked back to the door.

"Praise to the..." he said, and the door closed.

"I am Cantarita," said the woman. "And you are..."

"Confused," Zeke said. "Why is this guy hell-bent on my meeting you?"

"The Preacher is a little strange always, but he's backed himself into a theological corner of sorts."

"How's that?" Zeke asked, as he rubbed his hands together. The light through the windows did nothing to warm the place. He noticed that Cantarita was sitting upon a down sleeping bag. He would have liked to get in it.

"Well, I had no place to stay a while back. My boyfriend...well, that's another story. The Preacher took me in, said I could stay until spring or until life turned around, whichever came first; but then about a week ago he started looking at me strange and told me we had to sleep in separate rooms. I took this one for the light."

Cantarita waved her hand through the air, Rimbaud still in it, her thumb marking the page where she had been reading.

"I finally figured out I got the Ol' boy aroused. He thinks all men without women jerk off, which he doesn't approve of, except of course holy men who are supposed to be beyond all that carnal stuff. Sex outside marriage is also taboo. So he's kinda stuck. He can't take things in hand, so to speak, and relieve his frustration, but neither can he approach me."

She laughed, something Zeke realized he hadn't heard anyone do for a very long time. The last laughter he could remember hearing was his own when he told himself the Prufrock joke shortly after he moved to the Regency Arms.

"So," she said, "he's decided to pray for me a husband, which would make me completely taboo since there's that commandment about another man's wife, and thus effectively end his hunger for me since wanting another man's wife is beyond his wildest imagination."

She laughed again. It made Zeke warm, a little, and he could feel the corners of his own mouth turn up slightly, which also hadn't happened in a while.

"Poor guy," said Cantarita. "When he explained all this after I confronted him with my suspicions, I thought I'd bust I laughed so hard, but he was serious as hell."

"What happens now?" Zeke asked.

"I didn't really expect anybody to show up, of course," said Cantarita, "but, since you're here, maybe you could just let the ol' guy perform the ceremony. There's nothing official about it of course, no real license or anything, but it would put Preacher's mind at ease."

Zeke saw no harm and agreed. Besides, he owed the Preacher for the warm bed and meal, and maybe for his life. He realized his options had become severely limited by the time he entered the alley outside the warehouse. Zeke took Cantarita's hand and helped her to her feet.

She walked gracefully to the door, like a model walks a runway, Zeke thought, her steps all sexual innuendo and self-assurance, and summoned the Preacher.

****

The ceremony was brief. The old man read from the most worn Bible Zeke had ever seen, and Cantarita stood beside him, both arms wrapped around his one arm and her cheek resting against his shoulder.

When the Preacher came to the part about there being objections or holding one's peace forever after, he stood on his toes and craned his neck to see over Zeke and Cantarita, like there was a congregation behind them in the corner of the warehouse. There apparently were no objections.

"I now pronounce you man and wife," said the Preacher. "You may kiss the bride."

He seemed relieved as he walked away after Zeke and Cantarita kissed each other, long though decidedly without passion.

"Thank you," she said to Zeke after the door closed behind the old man.

They spent their honeymoon taking turns reading Rimbaud aloud.

Chapter 14

The next few days of their "marriage" passed peacefully enough. The Illuminations was the only book Cantarita owned. She found it on a bench near the art museum before the Preacher offered her sanctuary, and Zeke tired of reading it after his 15th time. So they talked.

Zeke admitted his name and, though his mother's voice echoed continually in his brain saying no lie is a good lie, he did just that. He told Cantarita a long, rambling tale of lost love and, with it, self-esteem. How he'd been a successful author until his wife was untrue, and how he had wandered the streets a lost soul since.

Cantarita laughed until she wept.

"I saw you weeks ago at the Regency Arms," she said. "Everybody downtown knows you shot your old lady and her boyfriend."

Zeke was embarrassed, more for being caught in a lie than for being a murderer. He could hear his mother clicking her tongue condescendingly in his mind.

"You are not afraid?" he asked Cantarita.

"You mean because I'm now the new Mrs. Reilly?" Cantarita grinned maliciously.

"No." Jake laughed out loud for the first time in weeks, since Eliot rolled in his grave, but nervously. This should not amuse anyone, he thought, and his head felt light. "...to even be in the same room with me, a killer."

"I've slept in the same room, in the same bed, with men far more dangerous to my health than you, Reilly. Men who kill for no reason greater than they want to."

Zeke grew more uneasy still at this last assertion. He was not sure he had a reason either.

Cantarita explained that she had been a hooker to Denver's elite for the last three years, that her pimp had underworld connections and, for reasons she did not explain, was looking for her even now with a small army of thugs, all with her bloody and painful murder in their pea-sized hearts.

"Do you have a plan for your escape, Reilly?"

"No. Do you have one for your escape?"

"As a matter of fact I do, and you can come along, although I warn you it is far more dangerous for you to travel with me than it is for me to travel with you." She patted his knee.

"When the weather lifts a little I intend to walk as quickly as I can to I-25 and thumb a ride. The trick is to get to the interstate without one of J.T.'s soldiers seeing me, and to get a ride without getting picked up by the cops because I think some of them work for him too, not to mention how much the boys in blue would like to get their hands on you. Then we head south. I still have people on the reservation, just outside Tuba City, Arizona. Once we get there I'm safe, and you're on your own."

Zeke dreamt again that night that everything was covered in spider web, as he had in the Regency Arms. It seemed like years ago and he felt very old. He dreamt that his own hands threw the stuff out in a line and he swung from it, away to the south. Only this time Cantarita was in his dream, and Cindy, and they were covered with white web as if covered in wedding cake frosting, stuck where they stood and asking him by the look in their eyes for some explanation as he flew by, an explanation he could not provide.

Chapter 15

"I ain't no Einstein," Zeke told himself the next morning as the clouds broke and Cantarita announced that they would leave in a half hour, after she talked to the Preacher and thanked him for his hospitality, for his Christian charity. She said those last words with no hint of derision in her voice. She said it like Zeke's mother would have.

Zeke felt helpless. He knew he was no judge of character, so must question how much he liked and trusted Cantarita; and he knew he was no judge of his own situation, so must question Cantarita's strategy; but he had no clue what else to do. In spite of his dreams and visions of the future, anything beyond tomorrow anyway had always been a problem for him. But right now even the concept, tomorrow, was beyond him. All he knew for certain was that he had to get out of town today.

He had been overcome several times in the last 24 hours with a rumbling deep in his bowels, a rumbling that sent mostly unintelligible messages to his brain but that intimated danger so strongly he swooned. In between bouts of dizziness and nausea he had an almost irresistible desire to run, anywhere, as fast as he could.

Cantarita came back holding the old man's hand. His eyes were red rimmed and he smiled so hard he beamed.

"God bless you," he said to Zeke and hugged him like a departing son.

Zeke and Cantarita left via the same door he had entered three days before. The plan was to walk as quickly as possible, without looking suspicious, to the west and then follow the fence that skirted the train tracks north to the nearest overpass and take that road to Interstate 25. The old man said it was roughly a mile and a half from the tracks to the highway through mostly run-down houses given over to squatters and crack-heads.

Zeke carried Cantarita's sleeping bag and Cantarita carried a paper bag with sandwiches the old man had made for them. They walked to the end of the alley. The world sparkled with two inches of fresh snow. Outside the shadows of the alley the world was almost unbearably bright.

"Oh shit," said Cantarita as she peeked around the corner. "Julio and J.T.'s brother, Zip Gun, are getting out of a car."

They ran back to the door. Cantarita started up the steps, but Zeke took her arm and pulled her toward the other end of the alley.

"Preacher will be better off if they don't catch us anywhere near him," he told her.

They ran across the street, then zigzagged to the next alley so no one coming out of the back door of the Preacher's warehouse could see them, although knew their tracks would give them away. They ran all the way to the street the old man told them had the overpass, then got on the sidewalk. They walked fast, but tried not to look too conspicuous, in spite of the sleeping bag. Cantarita said the bag merely told the world they were homeless, not fugitives.

At the top of the overpass Zeke looked back the way they had come. A black Lincoln with darkened windows rolled out of the alley where they had entered the street. Christ, he thought, I'm in a second rate movie written by a bad Poe imitator, all heavy handed symbolism and cliché, this car the ride of Death himself, and I am hanging out with a good hearted hooker to top it off. Zeke and

Cantarita ran down the other side of the overpass as fast as they could go.

Zeke could hear the cars on I-25, but he knew they could not beat the Lincoln to the road, and who knew if the fact that cars were going by would constrain Julio and Zip Gun anyway. The latter's name at least suggested a familiarity with prison, and, contrary to Zeke's perception of the place, maybe he wouldn't mind going back. Earl had told him once there were men for whom jail was home, a place where somebody at least cared about where they were, albeit perversely.

"I ain't no Einstein," he said to Cantarita, "but unless we can hide our tracks we're not going to make it."

Cantarita took an abrupt right at the bottom of the overpass and ran to the back door of a run-down, shotgun house like the railroad built for its employees in the thirties and forties. The door was not locked and they ran in, past two men sleeping on the floor, to a side room with a window, climbed out and ran to the front of the next house, up the steps and through the door, then to the side window again, through it and back to the alley.

"Hopefully," said Cantarita breathing heavily, "if they have to follow our tracks it will slow them enough for us to get to the interstate. We will have to get a ride right away or it's all over."

They crossed the next street without seeing anyone, then cut between two more run-down houses toward the end of the next block.

A roundish man with bald head and spectacles that looked too small for a human so large was standing at the curb with his penis in his hand. His other hand was on his hip in the classic stance of a man urinating. He smiled at them.

"Sorry," he said. "Didn't know anyone lived in these shacks. Just got off the road to see..." His voice trailed away.

Cantarita stood before him as he shook the last drops from himself and folded his penis back into his pants. She pointed at the red and rusting pickup truck that idled by the curb behind him. A large black Labrador hung its head out of the passenger window, watching and panting, its breath short bursts of fog on the air.

"We need a ride and very quickly," Cantarita said.

"I'm headed south," said the pisser, but Cantarita and Zeke were already climbing into the back of the truck. Zeke unrolled the sleeping bag and covered them.

"You'll freeze back there," said the truck's owner as he approached.

"Drive the fucking truck, now!" said Cantarita, peeking from under the edge of the sleeping bag.

The driver complied. Zeke could feel the truck roll toward the interstate, then accelerate down the ramp. They headed south at 75 miles per hour.

Chapter 16

"Now they're more surreptitious," said Bob Chance, the driver of the truck. "The dance of history has always been the dance of power. Big guys two-stepping up and down little guys' backs, but now the big guys have drugs and alcohol and TV and evangelical Christianity to control the masses."

He had talked nonstop since they got into the cab. Before they were even outside Denver's city limits their teeth chattered and Cantarita's lips were turning blue. Zeke had knocked on the window of the truck and they traded places with the dog, one Walt Whitman. Walt for short.

"Told you you'd freeze your ass off," were Bob Chance's first words. Cantarita was too cold to say anything back, but she flipped him off as Zeke helped her into the truck. She shook uncontrollably almost to Pueblo even with the truck's heater blowing full blast at her feet. She was between the two men now, her head resting on Zeke's shoulder, sleeping.

"I mean you hear how powerful the religious right is all the time, but truth is the politicos aren't going in fear of those zealots, not bending over backward to accommodate the Bible thumpers or anybody else among the great unwashed. They just smile a lot and tell the Christians they'll fix those heathens who abort fetuses and make obscene art and won't allow their kids to pray in school, but really the politicos, in service of the big guys, only make a token effort. Really they do little more than assert their empathy and pretend to do something. Maybe offer a bill here or there. Mostly give speeches. In all reality they're just happy the proles in the middle of the country, and of course in the South, have something to think about. The Christian proletariat, generally, is just happy to complain, which makes them feel important since their elected officials claim to see it their way, and shake their collective heads in disgust at the whole damn mess, since it certainly must be divinely sanctioned-the apocalypse come at last as it were_"

Zeke doubted it would matter to Bob Chance if he and Cantarita were there. He probably went on like this, ad infinitum, to the dog. Walt was probably happy to be outside, freezing his dog's ass off, but in happy silence.

The dog had spent his first hour in the back of the truck with his head hung along the passenger door, his nostrils flared, taking a big bong-hit of reality, as Chance put it: "Sensory information hitting what passes for his frontal lobe like ten thousand out of control freight trains."

The dog now lay curled on Cantarita's sleeping bag in one corner of the pickup bed shivering.

Zeke fell asleep with his head resting on Cantarita's as Chance ranted about the distribution of wealth, how a paltry percent of the population seemed to hold all the cards.

In Zeke's dream Walt the dog turned into a coyote, its fur sparking, its eyes red with flame and a frightening animal knowledge. The Earth moved.

Deep in Zeke's body a distant thunder rumbled.

Chapter 17

When Zeke woke up the sun was setting. The truck was headed west through tall pines and much snow on a two lane state highway. Zeke could see the brilliant pinks and blues of an ice cold sunset above the treetops just to the south of the truck's path. Bob Chance and Cantarita were singing with the radio, an old Supremes tune.

"Baby love, my baby love...." Neither obviously knew all the words and there was much off-key humming.

"Where are we?" asked Zeke when the radio started to crackle and snap too much for the music to be heard.

"Somewhere in the mountains of southern Colorado," said Chance. "I know a cheap motel just outside Durango that's always got vacant rooms to rent..."

"We don't have money for a room," Zeke interrupted. He and Cantarita had pooled their money at the warehouse. He had eighty-two dollars and she had forty. In a fit of connubial charity he had divided the money evenly and given her half in case they were separated, so neither would be caught totally broke.

"I know," said Chance. "Cantarita told me about your situation. I'll get a room with two beds. I always do. One for me and one for Walt Whitman, but he'll just have to sleep on the floor."

Zeke looked at Cantarita out of the corner of his eye. She winked at him.

"Uh...our situation," he said.

"Yeah. Good thing you found this little lady," said Chance, and he patted Cantarita's knee. "Sounds like she saved your life."

Chance looked at Zeke with genuine empathy in his eyes. "Like I was telling your wife, I lost everything right down to my self-esteem to a woman too. I shoulda shot the bitch," he said and slammed his hand against the top of the steering wheel.

Zeke nearly choked. What had Cantarita told him?

Cantarita was pursing her lips together so hard the chords in her neck stood out, as if trying to tell Zeke to keep his mouth shut.

"It was OK she took the money and the house, even if she was fucking the guy next door, a guy I worked with in the department, but the garden was unforgivable. Sure, the garden went with the house, but she called me up one day after the divorce to say she had something to show me, and when I got there several shirtless men were laying sod over where I had planted my garden for ten fucking years."

He hit the steering wheel again.

"Shoulda shot the bitch for that one, yes sir." Chance was talking to himself now.

"But you didn't, right?" said Cantarita. "You just took off like my Zeke here." She was looking at Zeke as she spoke. Zeke wasn't sure what he saw in her eyes: fear he would say the truth or sympathy. The thought it could be the latter made Zeke inexplicably sad.

Chance didn't answer. He drove the rest of the way to Durango in silence.

****

The motel's neon was partly burned out. MOTE ZAN the sign said in the dark, written on the air in pink light.

"Welcome to the Motel Zanzibar," said Chance as he handed Zeke the room key, then he left to find food.

Cantarita went directly to the bathroom and stood in the shower for a full 30 minutes. Zeke could hear her moan in the steam occasionally, even through the closed door.

66

She emerged in her long underwear, a farewell gift from the Preacher she told, just as Chance arrived with twenty take-out tacos, beer and a fifth of Jack Daniels.

Cantarita wolfed down seven of the tacos, all cheap meat and wilted lettuce, then crawled into the bed furthest from the door with a sigh and a smile.

Zeke and Chance remained at the small table, working on the rest of the tacos and drinking Budweiser and watching a baseball game, the Cubs and the Rockies. A tiny irony thought Zeke, thinking of his hats. When the tacos were gone Chance poured two plastic motel glasses half-full of whiskey.

"To the woman who saved your life and to the painful death of the bastard-motherfucker who wants to kill her."

Chance drained his glass. Zeke took a big swallow and shuddered and cringed. His belly burned. Chance poured himself another glass and replaced the swallow Zeke had taken from his. Chance raised his glass again.

"And may the wombs of the women who tried to kill us both smolder and grow moldy."

Chance drained his glass again, and Zeke took another gulp and shuddered and cringed again.

It had been a long time since Zeke drank alcohol. The last time was with Judy a few weeks before she died. They drank many glasses of wine one night when Marianne was in class. They giggled like kids, and Zeke had come closer than ever to touching her. He wanted to touch her, but also thought she wanted him to touch her, to take her hand, to kiss her on the mouth. But in the end he wasn't sure. Maybe it was only a wine-induced delusion, a wish so strong it seemed actually so.

"I ain't no Einstein," he had told himself and left before he had to pick up Marianne at school. He just drove around with a buzz in his pants, and in his head from the wine, and hollowness ringing like a bell in his chest where his heart was supposed to be.

He felt tears welling in the corners of his eyes. The memory, the beer, and the whiskey were an emotionally deadly mix.

Then his mind moved on to Marianne, and he wanted to cry for guilt, for feeling guilty at not feeling guilty.

"What the fuck, man," said Chance. He was looking at Zeke and there were tears forming in the corners of his eyes as well. "Let her go. Your ex is as good as dead."

"You don't understand," said Zeke, shaken anew by the irony in Chance's last assertion.

"But I told you, man..."

"No." Zeke hesitated. No lie is a good lie, said his mother. He wanted to confess, but he didn't.

"Suppose," Zeke said, "A man is guilty of something but feels no remorse whatsoever. What does this mean?"

"Guilt is relative," said Chance. "Life has become a postmodern novel. There's a whole lot of coming and going, but to what end? If an act takes place in a vacuum, where the actors have no values, no sense of right or wrong, where those around the actors may purport to believe in something but then tend to act contrary to those values in their everyday dealings in the world, then indeed how can there be such a thing as remorse?"

"I ain't no Einstein," Zeke said. "Nothing you just said makes any sense to me."

"Well let's take capital murder," said Chance. "Hypothetically, human life is sacrosanct in this culture, so murder is a crime not only against humanity but also against divinity, however you define it. Yet, people starve because other people have all the money, there are wars sanctioned by the very government that prosecutes the murderer, and the state sometimes even murders the murderer. So what are we to believe? Life is sacred, but then there is a long list of exceptions? Life itself becomes so relativized that it is ultimately as meaningless as everything else in this culture."

"So you think murder is OK then?" Zeke asked. Chance took a swallow of whiskey and opened another can of beer.

"No, I don't," he said. "If meaning as consensually arrived at does not exist, if God is merely another excuse for whatever we do, to kill or not to kill, then responsibility shifts to the actor. This is a shift fraught with risk, of course, at least in the absence of some kind of species-wide enlightenment experience don't foresee. Just think of all the assholes in the world you couldn't loan your car to, let alone trust with your life."

"So a man must decide if killing another person is justified and society should pay no attention?"

"No. We're talking about guilt here, about morality. The state will always punish those who kill, except those with money enough to beat the system of course, but remorse must be the actor's choice."

"Like I said, I ain't no Einstein." Zeke scratched his head. His words were beginning to run together. "Clarity. All I want is a little clarity."

"Clarity is always hard won," said Chance, "and then maybe it's only a singular form of delusion that rings like a church bell on a clear day. That clarity is the truth seems unlikely. Even if there is such a thing as truth, it's probably so far beyond our paltry species we could ponder and search 'till we shit blood and never see the light."

"Never see the light," Zeke slurred as if it were an antiphonal amen.

"The world is all perspective. Interpretation," said Chance and he pointed at the TV. "Take baseball. I see a bunch of simps in funny clothes making a fortune to do something inane. If I think about it, however, I see the late 20th century's secular version of the opiate of the masses, something for all those millions to focus on.

"An anthropologist I know, and hope to meet up with next week in Phoenix, probably sees the diminished remnant of a warrior cult, like those team sports the Meso-American Indians played, a sublimation of the warrior-ethos that is also a moderate redistribution of the wealth so ghetto lads have something to hope for, a small fortune for doing something inane. And look at this: the game comes complete with ritual and fetishes like the way this pitcher rubs the ball with both hands, kneads it like the sacred tit of some divine lover, or the primitive kinetic poetry of those strange hand signals the catcher flashes against the backdrop of his loins..."

Zeke laughed. Chance was on a roll now, his speech getting faster and faster.

"Or maybe Strauss the anthropologist sees a metaphor for all human endeavor under the auspices of late capitalism: all spit-sweat-whack-run-and-dive for an abstraction-points, the win."

"But the majority of us see only simps whose good fortune we envy," said Zeke. "They're doing something innocuous and, for all intents and purposes, without hurting a soul."

Chance leaned forward conspiratorially.

"But the difference between you and the majority is you think about it, right? Otherwise you wouldn't have asked me about remorse."

"I ain't no Einstein," Zeke said as his chin slipped lower, as it touched his chest. He slept where he sat until morning.

Chapter 18

Zeke discovered the source of Chance's loquaciousness, his nonstop harangue, the next day when they turned southwest at Cortez and headed for Arizona. After sausage and egg sandwiches purchased at the Cortez McDonalds, Chance offered them a handful of small white pills with a line across the middle. Zeke refused in spite of Chance's assertion that these pills would help his headache, Cantarita took three, just for old times' sake she said, and Chance threw back the remaining handful and chased them with coffee from the big Styrofoam cup he held between his legs as he drove.

"They speak any English where you're going?" he asked and wiped the back of his hand across his mouth.

"Of course," said Cantarita, "the reservation is not another country, though some there would like it to be. People my age and younger speak English anyway. My mother refuses. She speaks Navajo most of the time, a little Spanish when she has to."

"Won't use the language of the conquerors, huh," asked Chance?

"Something like that. She is a holy woman, a healer, a woman-of-the-trembling-hands. She says white words carry doubt and deceit on their backs and diminish her power."

"I have a friend in Phoenix, an anthropologist who did work with the Navajo and Hopi some years ago. He's doing a project of some kind with the Indians in Northern Mexico now, some renegade band living in the Sierra Madres who are trying to pry an old time subsistence from the mountains. Anyway, he'd love to meet your mother."

"She won't talk to a white man, not willingly, though she deals with the BIA authorities on the rez when she has to. She makes them use an interpreter."

"You speak Navajo or Spanish?" Chance patted Cantarita's knee.

"Only a little of both. Enough to talk to my mother and the other elders, but I didn't grow up on the rez so what I know I've picked up here and there on my visits."

"How about you, Zeke? You gonna have anybody but Cantarita to talk to?"

"I know a little Spanish, I guess, but that's from reading Neruda in translation, one of those with the Spanish version on the opposite page. I used to read the original for the music, the translation for what it meant, but spoken Spanish will probably go by too fast."

71

"Personally, I speak a little Spanish for much the same reason you do, so I can read the poetry, though I learned it in a classroom. The only other language I speak fluently other than my mother-tongue is academic-ese, but I've made a concerted effort to forget that language for the same reason Cantarita's mother refuses to speak English."

"You're a professor?" asked Zeke. His voice betrayed his surprise. He'd never been to college, but much like the rest of America, those who had been to college included, he had a vision in his head of what a professor is: part stereotype and part inflated myth-all tweed and single minded intelligence.

"Was. I quit the academy at the same time my wife quit me."

"What the hell is academic-ese," asked Cantarita?

"Oh, you know, the way those poor drudges talk who have gone to school half their fucking lives, people who get fucking PhD's in modern fucking American Literature. Good stuff, actually, but the price you pay includes acquiring the language."

"What separates this language from the way we're talking now," asked Zeke, "aside from the adjectives you just used?"

Chance laughed. "Well its characteristics aren't all linguistic. There's a certain slump of the shoulders the speaker has to achieve, and you have to stare at your shoes when you walk like you're deep in thought, like those loafers are the most meaningful constructs in the universe, a post-structural paradigm for human existence you're hoping to decipher.

"You can't look up no matter what. The moon waxes and wanes, the leaves turn, students jerk off in the bathroom then throw themselves from the roof in a failing-grade-induced frenzy, but you can't see any of it. You must look at your shoes.

"The next phase in achieving facility is to talk as if your body has disappeared. You use a non-corporeal pronoun like one and you quote people to beat the band. One of the last stages of achieving total fluency is to use et cetera as if it were the seed syllable of the universe, a mantra of indefinite, not to mention infinite, knowledge.

"Very few people in all the world understand this language of course, and of course when they speak to each other all parties look at their shoes and nothing else. Consequently, I'm convinced there is not a single speaker of this language anywhere who is not suicidally lonely."

The snow along the side of the road became less deep with each mile, then disappeared all together as they descended through the foothills. Chance talked nonstop. They could see the land flatten abruptly a few miles ahead and the road laid out straight over the high desert as far as the eye could see.

The truck flew down the last long hill and hit the desert floor at ninety. Cantarita held Zeke's hand, an act of fear not flirtation. Chance chased another handful of whites with a warm can of Budweiser he found under the seat when they stopped for gas at a junction just over the Arizona border.

Chance said his plan was to drop Zeke and Cantarita at her brother's house in Tuba City, then double back to this same highway and head for Phoenix. He planned to hit the city limits before nightfall. He talked about places he might stay as if thinking out loud.

"I could stay in the room over Digger's Pool Hall downtown, except for the fact that I got drunk with his wife one night and tried to kiss her. Tequila makes me hopelessly horny, or maybe it just messes with my vision so even a friend's overweight and overworked wife looks like a starlet. At any rate, I left town the next day since it does not pay to piss off a guy named for his knife technique. That was two years ago, but if she told Digger he'll still be looking to cut me up since men have extraordinarily long memories when it comes to such things. I can't blame him.

"There's another room at the back of a bar named the Shamrock a few blocks from Digger's where a big cross-dressing bartender named Queenie let me sleep a couple of times when I'd

73

had too much, but there's no shower so I couldn't stay more than a week. Even a preternaturally decadent fellow like me can't stand his own pungent fragrance after a week.

"I guess I'll have to go to May's, even though she'll put me to work. May is a 285 pound madam in Mexican Town. A really lovely woman, or as lovely as somebody who gets her money from young women selling their bodies to riff-raff can be anyway. In her defense, however, she's as close to family as most of her girls have, though admittedly the economic arrangement makes this version of familial bliss a tad perverse. But she keeps the books straight and pays the women well, and she protects them from her customers.

"I got belligerent with her myself once. I didn't, well, get to finish, if you know what I mean, and this whore told me my time was up. When you have your heart, hell your entire being set on that total release and it doesn't happen...well, anybody would get a little belligerent. I hollered at the woman who just sat there on the bed filing her nails and repeating, time's up. May came at what passes for a run for a woman of her size. She threw my pants at me and told me to get out. I threw them back and told her, stupid me, to go to hell.

"The next thing I know my nose is flattened across my face and I'm bleeding like the proverbial stuck pig. Then, with one swipe of her big hand, she knocked me out the door and down the steps.

"She picked me up by the back of my shirt, all two hundred thirty pounds of me, and I thought she was going to finish me right there, but she dragged me to the kitchen and cleaned me up and fed me some tripe soup and even gave me a job-fixing toilets, changing locks, painting over the bodily effluvia spattered on walls, things like that.

"That's where I'll go, I guess, I can make a little money if May will give me something over and above room and board..."

Chance didn't shut up all the way to Tuba City.

"Amphetamine autopilot," Cantarita whispered to Zeke.

74

Chapter 19

Cantarita's brother met them at the door of his clapboard house on the outskirts of Tuba City dressed only in a stained t-shirt. All the paint had peeled from the house years before and it was a weathered gray, the color of Indian desperation Cantarita had called it when they pulled up. The front yard held an old hand wringer style washer full of sand, and several bicycles without wheels or handlebars, and the remains of a wheel-less 1948 Dodge pickup on cinder blocks, and a rocking chair in pieces, and a sofa without cushions, and thousands of dry tumbleweeds thrust under and pushed around everything else.

Cantarita's brother, Francis, held his hand to his forehead the entire time he spoke to them as if it would fall off and his brain would be exposed if he let loose of it. His eyes were more bloodshot than any eyes Zeke had ever seen.

Francis agreed to take them to his mother's hogan west of town, but he said he had to find his car first. He had only discovered that he was in his own bed when they knocked on the door and he woke up in it. He wasn't sure how he got to his house or where he left the car. All he knew for certain was that it was not parked on the dirt street in front of the house.

He wandered back into the interior of the house as Chance said his good byes at the front door. He told Zeke and Cantarita to look him up at May's Boarding House if they got to Phoenix, then roared off in a cloud of dust as Walt Whitman barked madly at them out the passenger window.

Cantarita found Francis back in bed, asleep. She declared him unwakable and told Zeke they would probably go out to her mother's later that night. Then she went to the kitchen to see what food could be found. Zeke heard her cursing the mold and digging out dishes as he watched midget wrestling on an old black and white set, probably 1940's vintage judging from the cube-shape, with its rabbit ears wrapped in aluminum foil to help the reception.

"We're about to go back in time," Cantarita told Zeke as she handed him a plate of peanut butter sandwiches and a bag of chips. As if this hovel and its ancient television set weren't far enough removed from the postmodern world, thought Zeke. She went back to the kitchen and returned with two large glasses of milk and sat down on the couch next to him. Six very short women in tights, three to a team, hurtled each other across the screen.

"My mother lives in the old way, or as close to it as she can get at this late date. She lives in a hogan, a more-or-less round house made of wood and dirt, out on the high desert. No electricity or inside water, an outdoor shitter, smoke hole in the roof, the whole nine yards." One little woman on TV picked up another over her head and threw her out of the ring.

"How did you end up a hooker in Denver," Zeke said between bites? "I mean, if you don't mind my asking." The little black and white woman had bounced like a corpse, but now she crawled under the ropes, back into the ring, a trooper.

Cantarita smiled at Zeke, a half-smile that he could not read. Wistful? Sad even? But Zeke could see no hint of weakness in Cantarita's half-smile. No tears would come to her in this conversation, however painful. Zeke knew this like he knew all things that came in his dreams: a fact, though he did not know how he knew.

His body shuddered with memory. He had sat on this hole-filled couch before and stared at this beautiful Navajo face. He knew what Cantarita was about to say, and more, and it made him sad. He longed for the days when he could retreat into his hackneyed excuses for such feelings, when he could still pretend it was not happening. He was unsure whether his will power was weakening or the strange signals were growing stronger the further south he traveled, outstripping his ability to stave them off.

76

"Well, technically we are still husband and wife, Zeke Reilly, so I guess I can tell you what no one knows completely but me..." Three of the small women held a single one to the ground in the center of the ring, and they were biting her.

"I was born in a hogan very much like the one where my mother lives now. I was number eleven of twelve kids. When I was six years old, almost seven, the BIA decided my mother was unfit to raise those of us under 15, whether because we had an outside shitter and spoke only the old language or because my mother had taken up healing just before that is an open question.

"They took all of the younger ones to Utah and scattered us in foster homes. I was raised by a Mormon family in Salt Lake City. Good people really, though I found out later just how condescending their act of altruism was."

A tall man in a white suit climbed into the ring on the television. He threw the three small women off their victim and picked her up. He held her to his shoulder like she was a strange child, 3 feet tall but with breasts. The little woman hugged him as her savior.

"You mean, they took you in because you're a member of one of the lost tribes of Israel," said Zeke, conscious not to betray where this knowledge came from, from dream.

"Yes. They treated me well though, pretty much like they did their own kids: bought me clothes, drove me to school, helped me with homework."

"And you found your mother by accident," said Zeke more boldly. It was a flat assertion, a prompt. He had dreamt the answer, but he had also dreamt Cantarita's need to answer and she went on as if in a dream herself.

"When I was seventeen I ran into a Navajo man downtown, by accident. He was begging for money. He said, can you spare some change little sister? He referred to me that way because I'm Indian and younger than he was, but something clicked inside me. I'd been thinking a lot about where I came from, who I had been

77

before I was a Mormon adoptee. My adopted parents never answered when I asked, and in all fairness maybe they didn't know, not the particulars anyway.

"But when this man called me little sister I thought he must really be my brother and recognized me. As it turns out he was my brother, though he didn't know it when he asked for change, a coincidence that is not so extraordinary as it might seem. Many men from this reservation end up on those streets, drunk and with nowhere to go. When I told him my name, he cried. He was one of the older ones who was not taken by the BIA. He was sixteen when they took the rest of us away. He was homeless and a wino when I met him."

Cantarita looked at Zeke and her eyes were dark and hard. On the TV the man in white had blood on his suit. He set the little woman back in the ring and pushed her toward her opponents. He lifted her two team mates over the ropes as well and pushed them toward the center of the ring. All six tiny women collided in the middle and flew backward, a centripetal explosion of flesh. They writhed and groaned on the canvas as the man in the bloody white suit raised his arms as in victory, as if carnage were the whole point of the exercise.

"Your brother is dead, isn't he?" said Zeke.

"Yes. Almost all those left on the rez are. I went to see my brother in the part of Salt Lake relegated to his kind by the city fathers as often as I could sneak away, and he told me all their stories: knife fights, death by exposure, car wrecks, outright suicides. Then he died too. He got a cut on his foot and contracted gangrene. He told me that he did not want medicine, that his death was a sacrifice to the Gods of our people."

"Sounds like he just wanted to die," said Zeke.

"He did," said Cantarita. "The Gods were his excuse. The plural sounded like heathen blasphemy to me at the time, but I recognized, even as young as I was, that belief has nothing to do with his death. He had to die to quit hurting."

78

They watched the television and chewed in silence for a while. Wrestling had been replaced by a cartoon about impending ecological disaster. Young people with super powers were trying to stop some bulldozers that were ripping up a rain forest. The show was sponsored by a toy company offering a green slime that bounced thirty feet when slammed into concrete. It glowed in the dark.

"But what about those taken from the reservation when you were taken? Did they survive?" Zeke asked finally.

"Depends on what you mean by survival. I looked until I found them all, first through adoption records then through the BIA's own records that a friend had access to when some of those leads were dead ends. One brother is a deacon in the Mormon Church in Idaho, which is funny as hell in a way. He's a good man, although he wears that ol' Mormon condescension toward the lost tribe like a shirt. One is a fire fighter for the Forest Service, brave and honorable and strong. One sister is a waitress in Park City, Utah. Francis, my baby brother, you met. The others aren't as fucked up as he is. Sometimes I tease him that, for all his time away, he sure acts like a traditional reservation Indian. But the others are as lost as he is, in a way. Cultural orphans."

"How about you?"

"Yeah. Me too. I came down here after I found everybody else, and I thought my mother was an agent of the devil. I figured she had to be one of hell's own, what with those rituals she performs. I watched her work on a guy with gout my second or third night here. She pulled a bloody mass out of his foot with her teeth and I fainted. I never heard of such a thing, except in Mormon literature warning their youth about cults and devil worshippers. There were actually descriptions of just what she did that night.

"For a time, I figured the BIA was right to take us away from her, that at best, even though the guy she worked on that night was wholly healed of his gout and I saw her do nothing but good for people with her strange magic that whole first time I was here, she wasn't Christian which meant she was a lost soul and we would have been too. We'd have grown up heathens." Cantarita laughed, "Now look at me: hooker to mobsters."

"So when did you come to terms with what your mother is?" asked Zeke. It was one of the few answers his dream had not held, but he instantly lamented the pop-psych sound of the words.

"I don't think I have done that yet," said Cantarita, and her enigmatic half-smile returned. "We get along, but I don't claim to understand her. I have no frame of reference for what she does. My Mormon childhood gave me only demonic comparisons."

"Why do you come back then?" Zeke asked.

"I fled north in horror after a couple of weeks here, it's true. I met a seemingly nice Anglo guy with a big car who eventually pimped me out to any guy with fifty bucks. Then I ran from him to a man just like him, but with a little more upscale clientele, and then to another and another. I ended up doing rich men for the bastard who now wants to kill me.

"But I come back here every year. I tell whoever I work for that I'm on vacation, then book a room somewhere, last year it was Jamaica, just in case he gets suspicious that I'm not coming back, but I come here and just hang around until the desperation gets to me.

"It's not something I can explain easily. I tell myself it is so I can recognize true despair when I see it, so what I do for a living is justified. I mean, I'm not Francis and I do, usually, have nice things to wear and somewhere nice to stay regardless of how I earned the money to pay for it, but that's the American dream, right?"

"But there is more," said Zeke matter-of-factly.

"Now you sound like Beak, the old man my mother hangs out with, a shaman. He's always saying things like they're so." She laughed. "I've never figured out if he reads minds or is just an astute interpreter of the human condition, or if he's completely full

80

of shit, though to tell the truth he is right too damned often for it to be the latter."

Cantarita stacked their glasses on the plates and headed for the kitchen.

"This is home, isn't it?" said Zeke.

"Yeah," she said from the doorway. "Such as it is. I try to joke about it, that I come here because my mother-the-witch put some kind of spell on me to make me come back, that I'm a masochist who loves to have her nose rubbed in the shit that spawned her; but the truth is, in spite of the general hopelessness on the rez, there is something here that is a comfort, an atmosphere I think about when things get hard wherever I am."

Cantarita turned and walked into the kitchen. Zeke could hear the water running in the sink.

"Home is as good a word as any," she said over the noise.

****

The indoor swimming pool in Tuba City was filled with very large women and their Down's syndrome children. They splashed and laughed happily, all the picture of paradoxical grace in the water. They looked to Zeke like manatees with their young, and Cantarita was their mermaid, a goddess in a black swimsuit. Her dark hair was in a thick braid that floated behind as she swam laps from one end of the pool to the other in a lane demarcated with a rope and blue buoys.

A young man with eyes identical to Francis' eyes, bloodshot from corner to corner, had handed the keys to Francis' car through the door to Cantarita without saying a word. Then he had climbed into the cab of the broken down Dodge on blocks in the yard and gone to sleep.

"Hope he doesn't die," Cantarita had said as she looked at the sky. A low gray ceiling of clouds had settled over the desert. They were fat with moisture.

"The temperature in the 40"s and alcohol-thinned blood are not a good combination."

Their conversation about her past had made Cantarita restless and she said she wanted to swim, so Zeke drove her into town in Francis" starship-sized-early-seventies-model Buick.

Zeke had literally shivered at the sight of Cantarita's tight body in her swimsuit. Her nipples seemed to smile and point at him through the thin nylon, as did the small protuberance of her much used sex. Zeke wondered if a woman who had sex for pay for so many years could ever actually make love, or if all men were merely potential customers or potential pimps and potential abusers.

He watched the sweet bump of Cantarita's bottom move like a dolphins fin through the water for several laps, then turned his attention to the round women and their children in the shallow end to escape his growing hunger for her. Most of the mothers looked to be in their thirties or forties, and the children seemed to range from very young to teenaged, though their open and innocent faces tended to defy any specific age in years.

One pair of swimmers was obviously older. The one with Down's syndrome was well past her teens, if the sag of her breasts and the wrinkles around her eyes were any indication. The woman who pulled her through the water by her hands, like the mothers did with their children, was in her fifties. Like her swimming companion, the sag and wrinkles of her flesh told Zeke she was older than the other women, but her hair was also going white. In spite of the one swimmer's Mongoloid features, the two looked much alike and Zeke assumed they were sisters.

The sister without Down's syndrome stumbled as she pulled the other, and her sister's head crashed into her chest. The puller-by-the-hands went under water and came up spitting just as her sister found the bottom with her feet and came up spitting and choking too, her eyes wide with fright at losing hold of the other's guiding hands. For a single moment the two women were twins.

Their hair hung in their face and water ran from their mouths and noses. They coughed and pushed the water and hair from their eyes as mirror images. Then they laughed, simultaneously, and slapped the water into a boiling froth of pure joy.

Zeke longed for simplicity, for a keen awareness of all the boundaries of human existence: what was right beyond doubt and what was wrong, the proper path from the dangerous one, if indeed there was a choice, and, more than anything, some sense of purpose. He felt as if he were hurtling toward an unfathomable end, perhaps as punishment for killing Marianne and the plumber, perhaps for being stupid, perhaps for failing to understand this strange déjà vu.

"It must be Tuesday," said Cantarita, now standing before Zeke where he sat on a bench along the wall. She was dripping and shivering. "This group has come here every Tuesday for years."

Zeke's eyes went up and down her entire length against his will. Cantarita looked at his crotch, which was also doing things against his will, and laughed.

"Be careful," she said. "This union can't last much longer. I have to decide my future, and you will have to move off into your own."

Zeke knew this was true. He probably knew better than Cantarita, given his strange tendency to prescience, and the fact that his dream of her the night before had included his departure. The matter-of-factness of her statement made him sad, none-the-less, people moving with impunity in and out of each other's lives, mostly without even thinking about it, and he pictured Cindy in his imagination. Her forthright intelligence he could only admire, her strangely furtive bearing, her concupiscent mouth he would miss for the rest of his days.

Chapter 20

The back seat of Francis' Buick was big enough for Cantarita to stretch out on, and she did. She said sleeping through the whole experience was the only way she could stand Francis' driving, that all Indian men should name their cars and trucks "Death Wish," have it painted on the doors in day-glo orange paint, because that's how they drive.

Zeke understood exactly what she meant after only a mile. Francis had gotten out of bed at eight in the evening and agreed again, since he didn't remember the first conversation, to take them to his mother's hogan; but first he had to pick someone up at Gray Mountain, a small town just outside the reservation. Then he said he'd take them to the hogan via back roads from there since his mother's place was just the other side of the Little Colorado River due west of town.

They had hit the highway like Francis believed the big Buick really was a starship and Gray Mountain a distant galaxy. The car knocked and shuddered and Zeke could see the steering wheel, and Francis' hands and arms and shoulders, shaking violently in the green glow of the dashboard lights. The speedometer did not drop below a hundred until they reached a run-down bar just off the reservation. The car skidded to a halt in the dark parking lot. Zeke could see only two pickups parked just outside the door by the yellow light of a Miller High Life sign in the window.

Francis and Zeke left Cantarita asleep in the back seat and went in to look for Francis' friend. She wasn't there yet, Francis announced, and ordered two beers and two shots of tequila before Zeke could protest. When the bartender set those up in front of them, Francis told him to bring two more. He threw the shot back and had the beer two-thirds gone before the bartender returned. Then he directed Zeke to a round table in the middle of the room.

"Rose'll be here around 9:30," he said. "We can drink until then." He ordered more shots and beer after drinking his and the ones Zeke wasn't sipping on. The jukebox blared a whiny song about forgetting and drinking, and Zeke found himself humming along and tapping his fingers on the table, participating in the strange incongruity that is up-tempo honky-tonk: words to make you cry, a beat to make you dance.

"Hey white man," said a voice from behind Zeke. "You come here to drink with real men?"

"Don't turn around," said Francis between shots. "It's just Tom Big Bull and he's shit-faced. You turn around and he's gonna want to fight. Stoned or sober, that's not a good idea. He carries a knife in his boot that's damn near as big as he is."

"You come to hang out with little pussies like Francis, or you want to drink with real Indians, with warriors?" The man's voice boomed over the new song on the jukebox, a deep nasal twang about divorce and splitting the bedding. Down-tempo and wholly sad.

Zeke could hear a chair scrape as it was pushed backward on the decaying wooden floor and large, slow steps growing louder behind him.

"Shit," said Francis without looking at Zeke. "You might be dead." He ordered another shot and beer as the barmaid walked by.

Zeke sat facing the door and he could see Cantarita walking toward them with her fists clenched and a short, roundish Indian woman in tow.

"Let's go Francis," she said. She said it like a mother to an erring child.

The owner of the voice stood next to Zeke now, and the owner was huge. From the bottoms of his cowboy boots to the top of his Amax coal hat was about six and a half feet, give or take an inch or two. The man's belly hung over his belt a few inches, but there was no other fat on him that Zeke could see. His face was pockmarked and scarred and his big nose was nearly flat, signs of much violent engagement Zeke was certain, but he could not take his eyes off the man's hands. They were as big as skillets and belonged to what his Uncle Earl had identified to him enviously after a shoving match with a sailor at Coney Island years before as a born brawler. A man with hands that big was born to hit people his uncle had said, to break limbs and beat his own chest in victory. Such a man swayed next to Zeke now like a pine tree in the wind.

"So Little-White-Man-Fucker has come back to get some Indian dick, huh." Tom Big Bull reached out his skillet-sized hand and stroked Cantarita's breast.

Without thinking Zeke grabbed his beer bottle by the neck and swung it, back hand, with every ounce of strength he had. It hit Tom Big Bull squarely in the crotch and he dropped like a 300 pound sack of sand to the floor. His eyes crossed and he began to retch.

Zeke stood and turned to meet the commotion behind him. Two men approached with knives in their hands. Zeke growled like a dog and they stopped ten feet away. There was a puzzled look on both their faces. Tom Big Bull struggled to his knees and Zeke broke the beer bottle across his face. Blood Spurted from his nose. He was moaning on the floor in his own puke and blood as Zeke backed toward the door, the broken remains of the bottle extended toward the two men with knives, who still looked confused by what they were witnessing.

Cantarita and the others were already outside. Francis was flattening the tires on the pickup trucks with a knife and Cantarita and her companion were getting in the Buick.

Cantarita drove through the dark, her rage visible in the whiteness of her knuckles on the wheel, and her "countenance that would not unfrown itself." Zeke remembered this last from some poem or other, about a boy's mother he thought, and wondered

86

why Cantarita was so angry, and whether she was angry with him or with Francis or with Tom Big Bull or with men generally.

Francis and his friend had boisterous sex in the back seat. Her name was Rose Little Bird. She and Zeke were introduced as Francis unbuttoned her blouse. Cantarita seemed not to notice.

****

They turned down a two-track road off the dirt country road that crossed the Little Colorado. The first few flakes of snow were beginning to fall as they pulled up to what looked to Zeke like a mound of earth with light coming out of a door cut into its side and light and smoke seeping through a hole in the top.

"I didn't think it snowed in the desert," said Zeke, but Cantarita did not answer. She stopped the car and headed for the small square of light at the side of the mound. A blue Subaru and two pickups were parked along the two-track ahead of Francis' Buick. Rose and Francis stayed in the back seat, Francis' head resting on Rose Little Bird's bare chest.

Zeke caught up to Cantarita and grabbed her arm. She took it away indignantly.

"You mind explaining to me why you're mad?" asked Zeke.

"What did you think you were doing, Zeke Reilly? A lot of men have grabbed this tit, many less gently than Tom Big Bull. Did you think you were defending my honor, or some such chivalric bullshit? My honor was gone a long time ago, besides I can kick his big ass and yours simultaneously."

She had been poking Zeke in his chest with her forefinger as she spoke and he thought for a moment she might prove her point; now she grabbed his arm and drug him through the door of the hogan. The doorway was slightly shorter than Zeke and he bumped his head hard. Cantarita giggled like a young girl with a vicious kinetic sense of humor. Zeke rubbed the knot on his forehead.

"Now we're even," she said.

The inside of the hogan was warm. There was a fire in a raised stone circle in the middle of the large single room, and smoke floated up and out the hole in the roof. The room was filled with a soft red light and shadows moved up and down the walls.

Three men began to beat drums as Zeke and Cantarita entered, softly and not exactly in unison. Zeke felt dizzy for a minute, but got his equilibrium again through his tried and true method, denial, which seemed to be working again, at least for the moment. When he could see clearly again, Zeke noticed a naked girl of 9 or 10 lying on her back on blankets not far from the drummers. The child looked frail and frightened. A woman, Zeke assumed was the girl's mother by her worried expression, held the child's hand. A man, maybe the father thought Zeke, watched the drummers sternly with his arms crossed.

An old Indian man with a blue bandanna tied around shoulder-length white hair watched the proceedings from a few feet away. He seemed to direct things as much as observe them. Zeke saw him nod at the drummers and the beat quickened, became exactly synchronous, each man's stroke every man's stroke. Denial failed and Zeke's disequilibrium returned with a vengeance as the old guy nodded at the man he had assumed was the girl's father; he nearly swooned as the man began to chant in low rhythmic tones. The singer lifted his hands and his face toward the smoke hole.

An old woman in traditional dress and long gray braids and bent at the shoulders came in the door of the hogan. She hugged Cantarita who, not very tall herself, had to bend over to reach the old woman. Cantarita made hand gestures toward Zeke and said something in Spanish, but the old woman did not look at him.

She walked to the child and knelt next to her and held her wrinkled hands a few inches above the girl's naked body. Her hands began to tremble and she moved them up and down the girl's length for several minutes. Zeke's balance returned, but now he was zeroed in on the old woman as he had zeroed in on the priest at Judy's funeral. He could see each tremor, hear her whisper soothing syllables of a language he had never heard before, at once harsh and mellifluous as oral honey, vaguely pleasing and vaguely ominous; he could feel the current that moved back and forth between the old woman's palms and the girl's small body.

The woman's hands stopped above a spot halfway between the girl's navel and her bare pubic bone. Her hands hovered and shook there, and Zeke knew it took all of her strength to hold them above that spot. Then the old woman touched the girl with her right hand at that place over which her left hand still trembled. Her right hand shot out like a snakes head and plucked a quarter-sized, deformed creature from the girl's body. Zeke could see it clearly. It looked like a small, featherless bird, but without wings or legs, just a bleeding mass with a beak and an eye that made him take a half step back. Zeke could also smell the creature clearly, and it smelled like death. The woman threw the thing into the fire and there was a small popping sound like a cork being pulled from a bottle but that Zeke heard as a distant, angry roar; then a blue sizzle and a blue puff of smoke floated out the hole in the roof of the hogan. The drumming slowed.

The old woman and the girl's mother helped the child to her feet and wrapped her in a blanket with geometric designs and stick figures on it while the old man talked in the chanter's ear. The chant changed. Zeke thought it sounded dirge-like at first, but with an urgency to match the drums. Now there was a lightness that approached exuberance. The chanter's voice rolled up and down a five toned scale, in a key Zeke did not know existed. The drummers beat faster and faster again, and louder. The chanter's voice rose too, like an operatic tenor trying to reach the farthest seats with the same tidal wave of sound as the front row. Then, without warning, the chant and the drums stopped.

Zeke had felt bodiless by the end of the ceremony, like a breathing presence, like pure vision and hearing and smell. When the music ended he shrunk back into his corporeal self, but he still surged with raw energy, with power, like he could pull the place down with a single thought, like he could not only feel the very heart strings of God quiver, as Judy had so poetically referred to his gift, but make them quiver. But the feeling passed quickly and then he felt nothing but tired.

****

Cantarita stood at the door as the participants filed out of the hogan. She seemed to know them all and said a few words to each person, hugging the women and children. The old man in the blue bandanna hugged her too, kissed her cheek and whispered in her ear. Then he looked back at Zeke, who was sitting on a wooden chair by the fire wondering what he had witnessed, and smiled. Cantarita looked at Zeke too, clearly puzzled.

Francis and Rose had come in from the car as the last participant in the ceremony left and were now asleep against a far wall of the hogan wrapped in each other's arms. Cantarita's mother ladled water into a cast iron pot from a large barrel near the door, and Cantarita sat down on the ground next to Zeke's chair.

"Beak told me we are both here for a purpose," she said. "The old S.O.B. is always talking in riddles, but I found out a long time ago it doesn't pay to ignore him."

She put her hand on Zeke's leg. "So what's our purpose here, Zeke Reilly?" She wasn't joking. She asked the question like she meant it. Her eyes told Zeke she meant it.

"Maybe the old man is just making some esoteric observation about the general human condition; maybe he thinks we all breathe for some cosmic reason; maybe...." Zeke intended to lapse into his old habit of making a joke, like he had done whenever Judy raised the mystical issues she took so seriously and that alternately bored and scared the hell out of him, but it came out all exhaustion and mock snide.

"It doesn't work that way down here Zeke. No abstract pieties. Nothing is said or done, at least when it comes to people like Beak, and like my mother for that matter, unless there is some larger reason, a bigger scheme of things. I can't always tell what that scheme is, but I sense it's there. It's like those larger reasons hang invisible on the air down here."

Cantarita pulled her knees up and rested her chin on them and stared into the fire.

Cantarita's mother made them a kind of porridge. It had a gruel-like consistency, but she added butter and honey and Zeke pronounced it delicious.

The old woman still had not looked directly at him, but she smiled when he said the word.

"It's a cognate," said Cantarita.

"*Delicioso*," Zeke said in the old woman's direction, but she ate from her bowl and still did not look at him.

Cantarita's mother hummed the same set of four notes over and over by the fire as Zeke fell asleep under wool blankets.

****

Zeke was awakened in the night by sounds near him. The hogan was dark except for the glow of embers from the fire pit, and he could hear the deep human breathing of sleepers across the room, but someone stood over him.

He started to speak, to ask who it was, but then he smelled Cantarita, her subtle female scent. She moved between him and the small stream of smoke that rose through the hole in the ceiling, that headed out into the stars that shone beyond. By her silhouette he could tell that nothing hung on her shoulders but her hair, long and loose.

Cantarita knelt next to him and pulled back the blanket. She ran her hand down his face and his chest and his groin, held him there until he was an arrow of solid flesh, then she swung her leg over and settled onto him. Zeke entered the warmest place he had ever been, or would ever be, in his life.

91

Chapter 21

When Zeke awoke in the morning, neither Cantarita or her mother were in the hogan. Francis and Rose snored gently, in unison, against the far wall. He waded through the foot of snow that had fallen in the night to the two-track. The women's footprints had led here. The Buick was gone. As Zeke pissed on the road he could see a blue pickup truck moving slowly through the snow up the trail toward him.

Beak pulled up as Zeke zipped his pants. "Get in," said the old man in concise, almost too exactly enunciated English. "I'll buy you breakfast."

They rode in silence to a small cafe on the edge of Gray Mountain. It had once been a railroad dining car and was decorated with old kerosene lanterns and pictures of trains. They sat in a booth and the old man ordered steak and eggs and coffee for both of them.

"You have the sight, don't you," said Beak after the waitress poured them coffee and went to the kitchen to place their order. "You have dreams. Not the kind white people talk about when they really mean wishes, but the kind that portend something. You probably also have visions, which are the same as the dreams, more or less, but happen when you're awake."

"What makes you think so?" asked Zeke. He did not mean to be coy, but the same uneasiness he felt when Judy had talked about this subject washed over him. Some part of him just wanted to pretend the experiences never happened. Beak leaned toward him, his arms resting on the table.

"I won't give you some inscrutable Indian sorcerer story like half the young tourists come down here in search of. Let it suffice to say we are the same, you and me. The only difference between us is that I live in a dying culture that recognizes, in a systematic way even, these experiences as real, and you live in a dying culture that doesn't."

Zeke wasn't sure what the old man wanted, but the fact that he seemed to know about his strange experiences made Zeke uneasy at a variety of levels, not the least of which was that only Judy had known about his strange experiences. Now that bond that had seemed at the very least sexually tinged, the shared secret, seemed violated.

Beak sipped at his coffee. The waitress returned with huge plates of rare meat and eggs and potatoes fried with onions and peppers. Neither man spoke until they were pulling out of the parking lot and onto the road. Beak turned south and drove through Gray Mountain. Cantarita's mother's hogan was in the opposite direction.

"There is something I want you to see," he told Zeke, "over there," and he pointed toward the mountains.

The snow that had fallen the previous night had melted off the highway and turned to slush along the shoulders of the road; but after twenty-five miles or so they began to climb out of the desert and into coniferous forest, first scrub cedar then ponderosa then Douglas fir, and the snow got deeper with every mile. The old man drove the pickup through an open gate on a deeply rutted and rocky road that went west off the highway and up a ridge. After ten minutes of violent rocking and bouncing, Beak climbed out to lock his truck's front hubs in and proceeded for twenty minutes more in four-wheel drive. Zeke was thrown from side to side and bounced up and down the entire way. Beak seemed to ride the bumps like he was on a surf board. He just dipped with the troughs and rose with the swells.

When they reached the highest point on the ridge the old man stopped the truck and pointed to the south. A white peak stood head and shoulders above the mountains around it in the distance.

93

The only sunshine as far as Zeke could see was glistening on the summit as if the mountain itself tore a hole in the sky.

"Where we are right now is holy ground, and that peak is holy ground. The holiest for some of my people. It is where the world began and it is where the world will end. We will have a visitor here in a little while."

So much for the inscrutable Indian act he promised not to inflict on me, thought Zeke.

The old man climbed out of the truck. He instructed Zeke to look for firewood and began to clear a circle of snow ten feet across with a coal shovel he took from the back of the pickup. Zeke had intended to ask about this visitor, just who the hell would come way out here and for what reason, but after a few minutes in the snow he just wanted to get the fire going. His feet were wet and numb. Besides, the possible answer had an ominous feeling about it Zeke could not quite interpret. There had been no vision, or any dream that he could remember, about this particular situation, but his body hummed with a knowledge for which he as yet did not have language. But that knowledge carried darkness on its back, not exactly evil perhaps but something damned unpleasant, this much he could feel.

There was a fire pit made of large rocks in the center of Beak's shoveling that had held many fires judging by the rocks' blackness. There were four larger stones, worn smooth by many sitters, around the fireplace, one at each point of the compass. The old man retrieved a can of white gas from behind the pickup seat and soaked the wet wood Zeke had thrown in the fire pit with it. He threw a match and the fire started with a minor explosion, then settled into flames eating the wood as it dried.

"A little trick Tonto learned from the Lone Ranger," said the old man.

Beak directed Zeke to sit on the northern seat facing the mountain to the south. Zeke propped his feet close enough to the fire for his shoes to steam. The old man squatted on his haunches before the stone seat to the west and stared into the fire.

Zeke's feet warmed and dried quickly. The fire burned to embers. Zeke built the fire back up with the wood he'd piled nearby. The fire burned to embers again, and Zeke restored it with more fuel.

When the pile was gone, Zeke gathered more wood. Then he gathered more when that pile was gone, and still the old man did not speak, did not move, did not take his eyes off the flames.

Toward late afternoon the clouds began to break and the sun raged on the western horizon, set the southwest face of the peak on fire for the few brief minutes of the late winter sunset, and then it was dark. Beak still squatted before the fire. Zeke noticed that the old man's eyes were dark too, that they reflected no light at all from the flames.

The moon would not rise until late, although Zeke the city boy did not know it, and the only things he could see were the rocks and snow within the short circle of the fire light, and the stars. There were billions upon billions here like Zeke had not seen for many years. In the city there are no stars at all, and indeed no one looks up in the city, day or night, because there is nothing to see or because they are too focused on traffic and their own small thoughts or because even the once vestigial urge has now left them completely.

Years before, when Zeke came west, he had fallen asleep in a terminal somewhere in Iowa and missed his bus, so he had to hitchhike. He had walked to the edge of that little farm town by dusk, then walked beyond it into the dark when he could not get a ride. Once outside the influence of street lights he had looked up and gasped at what he saw, awestruck and, inexplicably, more than a little afraid. Someone stopped then to offer a ride and he had refused. He lay on his back at the margins of a cornfield and stared into the mouth of the universe all night.

He stared up at the stars now until they appeared to move as a single constellation, a magnificent order, a nearly comprehensible perfection. For a few minutes he believed there was a reason he was here, that the old man must be right. Purpose. Certainly the universe was a manifestation of purpose, and he would know soon, would be beyond doubt. Certainly Marianne and the plumber did not die for no reason at all. When Zeke's neck hurt unbearably he lowered his head and closed his eyes. The stars moved still, as orbital bliss, in his brain.

Then he tried squatting like Beak between his stone seat and the fire. Within only a few minutes his calf muscles were knotted and his knees ached, but he leaned back against the rock and managed to stay in the same position as the old man. He stared into the flames, at the shifting colors of redness in the fire's embers. Contrary to what he saw in the sky, this was the dissolution of all order, chaos, infinite and inevitable. A wave of peace had washed over him as he stared into the sky; now he felt a comparable dread. An ominous shiver shook him. This was a fear without cause so far as he could discern, but a fear that transcended any he had experienced in his life. He had no name for it, though Death came closest, but there was something darker than even death in how he felt: a blankness ten times blank, an emptiness that was as big as the sky, and it was everywhere, inside of him and out. This, now, must be the recognition of evil, he thought.

He pulled his gaze abruptly from the fire and turned his head to the west. His eyes met the lightless eyes of the old man who was now looking directly at him. The old man's head turned slowly toward the east, and Zeke's did too as if the old man's gaze pulled Zeke's with it.

A coyote stood at the edge of the light. It was looking at Zeke. Its eyes glowed red as the fire itself, and its coat glowed as if it were aflame. The coyote was there a second only, then turned to the east and disappeared into the dark. Zeke stared after it filled with a nearly overwhelming animal sadness.

****

They rode down the ridge in silence. Beak concentrated on the rough terrain in the dark. Zeke was too depressed to talk.

The old man had dumped snow on the fire right after the coyote bounded, or flew, Zeke was no longer sure, noiselessly away. Zeke had been unable to do anything but stare after the creature, and the old man had to grab him by the arm and pull him toward the truck.

When they bounced onto the highway and headed toward Tuba City, the old man apologized.

"I shouldn't have brought you here," he said. "Made Coyote sad."

Zeke didn't need to be told. He had felt the animal's despair himself. "But why?" he said.

"He didn't understand you either at first, so I don't feel so stupid. I knew there was something about you that I couldn't quite grasp, but I told myself that you white people are just strange, something we Indians can't completely understand."

They rode in silence for several miles. Zeke was shaking with déjà vu and falling farther into depression. Knowing what was about to come made him feel worse.

"I think white people's strangeness has to do with death," said Beak finally. "My people can touch death. We do it all the time in ceremonies. Death has a face, a form, and we can grapple with it, be consumed by it, even serve it if we are perverse enough. But we never take death for granted. Whites go even beyond taking it for granted. They pretend it does not exist, even in the face of all evidence to the contrary.

"Say a Mexican runs over a jack rabbit on this very road. He crosses himself like mad." Beak rolled his eyes upward and made the sign of the cross over and over so fast his movements were

97

spastic. In the dashboard lights he looked eerie, like a ghost, to Zeke.

"At least a Mexican respects death enough to fear it," said Beak, but then their tribal roots are very old and were only assaulted a relatively short time ago, in Indian terms anyway. "A white man, even a good Catholic, hits a rabbit and curses the blood on his tires and opens another Coors."

A jack rabbit jumped from the edge of the road and Beak had to hit the brakes and swerve to miss it. He laughed and there was something cruel in his voice to Zeke, almost brutal.

"I spent a couple of years of my youth trying to understand your race. I read your philosophers from Plato to Sartre, and could not stomach those macabre French guys who came later, not enough to read a whole book; but I must admit I didn't get much from any of them, confusion and amusement sometimes, but little else. Now here you are, and I finally get it. Death.

"A paradox, white people pretend it doesn't exist at all, but white people serve Death. Like I said, Death has a face for my people, attends our ceremonies, dances and sings with us, but in a way it is more omnipresent for your race. It's in your machines, in the toys you give your kids, in your square houses made of nothing remotely resembling the Earth...but Death is unacknowledged."

"So if my race is lost, why did you bring me here old man?" Zeke asked. He knew the answer, but somehow it had to be said.

"To save the planet." There was no hint of irony or grandiloquent self-possession in Beak's voice. It was simply an assertion.

"You see, people like me, like Cantarita's mother, are engaged in a great battle. Before tonight I thought our fight was merely with dark forces that manifest themselves as the petty but destructive machinations of so-called Western Civilization, a daunting enough enemy, and with a few of our own kind who are selfish, the perverse ones. But now I see our battle is with Death itself, that your race has already lost completely, surrendered to Death." The old man seemed smaller and much older than before to Zeke.

"Explain how the hell you saw all that tonight," he said.

"I brought you here because you have the sight. I thought your strangeness toward it was merely a result of cultural indoctrination, which is mostly true; but Coyote did not confirm your gift and offer me a way to bring you to our aid in this spiritual war as I had expected. He grew sad, and angry with me, because of the blood on your hands."

Zeke was silent now. The depression he had settled into seemed to preclude speech. He had heard all this anyway.

"Don't get me wrong Zeke. All living creatures are bathed in the blood of their fellows. Me and Coyote much more than most. I am, after all, a warrior. The results of what I must do in my cause are sometimes hideous to behold, but both Coyote and I know why we kill, and we never do it without remorse, even when what we have killed is evil itself.

"You, Zeke Reilly, are the guy in the car. The deaths you are responsible for are as senseless to you as the rabbit's on the highway, completely meaningless, just so much blood on the tires."

The old man sighed. Now he looked more than small and old to Zeke. He looked tired to his core, exhausted, maybe nearly dead himself.

"If one with the sight can achieve such apathy, then the odds of our survival have gotten very long indeed."

He turned to Zeke. "How the hell can a man breathe if death is a meaningless malaise, the same meaningless malaise he calls life?" There was no bitterness in his voice. If anything, Zeke heard desperation. Then the old man seemed to gather what strength he had left. He strained to sit up straight as if it hurt, pulling himself up with the steering wheel, and laughed like a madman.

Chapter 22

The sun was a thumb's width above the horizon when Zeke climbed out of Beak's pickup truck. The Buick was still gone, or gone again. Zeke didn't know which.

"I didn't ask for these dreams and visions," he said as he stepped to the ground. "If it's any consolation, I've considered dying several times since...to lie down and never get up, to dream the monochrome dreams of rocks and dirt, looks pretty good sometimes."

The truth was, self destruction had only occurred to Zeke recently. The first time was while drinking with Bob Chance in the Motel Zanzibar. The second was on the trip down the mountain just now. The realization that it all meant nothing, the random deaths, those for which he was responsible but all others as well, and his flight and the risk of jail and losing Cindy after he only just found her and all this damned feeling of being so insignificant and stupid. The list went on and on.

Certainly the ominous force he felt behind everything was Death. He had known it in some recess of himself all along; it was a sleeping worm in his own soul he could not quite rouse to show him the fatal truth of his life, of the universe itself, but whose tiny warped mind he could always almost read. And now Beak had confirmed it. He could look over Death's shoulder once in a while to glimpse Death's gruesome cards, but so what? He was an agent of Death himself, apparently unable to control his own hands and mind, and according to Beak his entire race was capable of such evil. What other word could he use to describe his lack of affect, his race's lack of affect?

Beak laughed and slapped the seat of the truck. He looked himself again, neither tired nor, except for his white hair, all that old.

"First, I wouldn't make too many assumptions about the dreams of rocks and dirt, let alone what happens to us when we die, but shirking the sight, let alone your life, is pure chicken shit. Just because you don't fit the purpose I thought you did doesn't mean you don't have one. It is true there are a lot of people on this Earth who are as good as dead and would do us all a favor if they just got the hell out of here, but in spite of everything that happened last night I can't believe even a stupid white man with blood on his hands can't find something worthwhile to do with this gift."

The pickup lurched forward and Zeke's door closed with its momentum. The old man swung his truck around between clumps of sage brush and soap weed, waved, and drove back toward Gray Mountain.

Smoke was rising from behind the hogan and Zeke went around to see who was up, hoping it was Cantarita's mother. His interior was a cocktail of certain doom and untranslated foreboding, but he had not eaten anything since his steak and eggs breakfast the previous morning and he hoped the old woman would fix him some food.

Instead he found Cantarita, naked, bending over the fire. Only patches of snow remained, but the night's chill was still on the land. Cantarita was wet and steam rose from her skin. She looked like an apparition in the low light.

The sight of her breasts swaying and steaming as she worked over a large pot on a grate above the fire pushed most of Zeke's exhaustion and depression out of him and filled him instead with desire. Amazing, he thought, that the weight of the apocalypse could lift at the sight of a naked woman

"There you are," she said. "Been out chasing Indian pussy with that crazy old man, I suppose." She laughed and stood up with her hands on her hips. "Come here, Zeke. You stink."

She led him to a five foot by five foot wooden stall enclosed on three sides and told him to take off his clothes. The erection that Cantarita's beautiful naked body had engendered wilted like a late fall flower in the cold air.

She ladled water from the big pot on the fire into a tin basin and poured it over Zeke and handed him soap. He lathered and she rinsed him. He shivered as steam rose from his skin, but his penis stood at attention again.

"Damn," said Cantarita when she saw him from the front, pouring warm water over his embarrassingly proud little brother in his pink helmet and pulsing chutzpah. "Men will never cease to amaze me."

She bent over and kissed him there and they made love standing in the stall, quickly. Their breath swam together, a single bright fish on the air, for a few moments, then they were finished.

When they were dressed and warming themselves by the fire Cantarita told Zeke he had to leave soon. Her mother had put a spell of protection on him the day before, after Tom Big Bull and two other men came by looking for him.

"She said she sensed danger for you far bigger than some big mouth Indians with knives. Maybe it has something to do with your trouble in Denver, Zeke."

She reached into her coat pocket and handed him a roll of bills. "The divorce settlement," she said.

She smiled her half-smile again and Zeke felt his sadness return, the same sadness that the coyote had brought with him, that Cantarita had momentarily dispelled. But he knew without her mother's warning that he had to leave. The sense of foreboding that had mixed with his depression like volatile chemicals the moment the hogan came into sight was even stronger now. Whatever his culpability, his failure to feel remorse for the murders or an

102

adequate purpose for his so-called gift, he still feared prison worse than death and a picture of his Uncle Earl broken spirited in Attica flashed through his imagination.

"Where did the money come from?" Zeke asked. "I thought we split what we had in Denver."

"I went to see a friend of Beak's at the tribal credit union today. He is a man beyond reproach, as close to uptight even as an Indian gets. But he hates white people in a way that borders on racism, and I asked him if he could access some of J.T.'s accounts. I happen to have the numbers.

"So he set up a series of accounts around the country and moved some of J.T.'s money all over the place until it wound up here, in my mother's name. I took only a couple of thousand dollars that J.T. owed me because I don't want to give him any more incentive to find me than he already has, but the old guy at the bank thinks we bankrupted another cruel white man. He was so pleased I thought he was going to dance on the desk."

Zeke squeezed the bills in his hand.

"Well I can't say I don't need it. I've tried hard not to think about how I was going to eat when what little I have in my wallet is gone. Thanks," he said and put the roll in his pocket.

"So where are you going?" he asked Cantarita.

"Nowhere, for now. I need a rest, and besides, my mother is getting older. She's slower and more hunched over than when I was here last, and I worry she won't be around one of these times, though it could be some kind of sorcerer-woman trick. I think she wants me to take over her practice." Cantarita laughed. "Imagine, me a healer. Puller-of-bloody-masses-out-of-Indians."

"There might be more to it than that," said Zeke.

"There you go, sounding like Beak again."

They hugged then and kissed passionately, sadly. Then Zeke slept wrapped in Cantarita's sleeping bag, folded in the sweet smell of her.

103

At noon Francis came back with the starship-sized Buick to take Zeke to Phoenix. Cantarita had promised Francis a hundred dollars for his trouble. How she knew Zeke must go south she told him she did not know, but he must. She told him so, emphatically.

Zeke told Cantarita that he loved her, and he meant it. They had been lovers a few times, even husband and wife since Denver, but he did not love her in that way, not that he had a clue what that way would feel like in spite of what he thought was a small taste of it with Cindy. But love was the right word.

"You are here for a purpose," he told Cantarita, and he knew this beyond doubt. He wiped a tear from the corner of her eye, then one from his own.

A little more than an hour later the Buick passed the two-track turn to the ridge, where Zeke had seen the coyote with Beak the night before, at 120 mph.

Zeke and Cantarita never saw each other again.

Interlude

Cindy Sweet Stuff's phone sex method was simple. It was so simple, she told her employees when she trained them, she wondered why no one had thought of it before.

The key was language she told them: you offer the client unlikely metaphors to heighten his fantasy-your mouth on him is like an oceanic storm, vortical and strong, cyclonic, a violent swirling sucking that takes his breath away and makes him fear his whole body will be pulled into your mouth-but you still use those taboo words that serve to keep the experience grounded in the real, just enough: cock, pussy, clit, asshole.

The accouterments, the sauce and spices, are things like setting. An unlikely place, for example, makes for danger-of-being-caught for some and exhibition for others: over a shopping cart in the nearest Safeway parking lot on a Tuesday afternoon, at the caller's parent's house and in his parent's bed while the folks

104

play backgammon in the kitchen, in the library between stacks at story time, in weightlessness aboard the space shuttle Endeavor (think of the thrust, Cindy loved to pun when she used this setting with a client, a joke most of them were too hormonally enraptured to hear).

Cindy also told her employees that her method allowed for sexual paraphernalia: the traditional whips and handcuffs and blindfolds, but also power tools and kitchen utensils, though these were obviously dangerous. The very unlikelihood of such appliances as sexual devices tended to make them alluring, but Cindy's only hard-and-fast rule was nothing gruesome, and some of her clientele were all too drawn to the bleaker roads of desire without the suggestion of electric drills and can openers.

Never encourage these guys to do terrible things, violent and hurtful things, to a woman's body, even in their pathetic imaginations, she told them. No woman should have to endure a rape fantasy of any variety, power tools in- or ex-cluded, for any reason, profit included.

Cindy had also discovered that clothing could enhance the caller's imaginative scenario, since clothes represented the person who wore them out in the real world. Like power tools, however, this affectation had its darker side as well.

Cindy warned her employees: cop uniforms and the pedestrian maid outfit are popular, one side or the other of the authority game as it were, but you'd be amazed how many requests there are for sister's panties or Aunt so-and-so's blue night gown.

Incest is one thing, and you must decide your own comfort level with such things since there are complex psychological questions here for us all, not to mention complex questions of authority and submission, of the differential power arrangements in family relationships, and I personally draw the line at consent as opposed to coercion since I insist all parties in these guys' fantasies remain adult and therefore ostensibly responsible for their own actions, although that line between consent and coercion might be an arbitrary one in the end too...but, once, a client asked me for his mom's apron. OK, I said, I'm in your mom's apron and nothing else and we're in the kitchen...No, he told me, I'm in my mother's apron. Go figure, said Cindy.

At the end of every training session she always reiterated that language remained central to their customer's gratification, to their calling Cindy Sweet Stuff's Phone Sex Service again, to their customers referring them to their friends.

In the beginning was the word, she liked to say, and God had no idea to what ends it could, and would, be used.

Part Three

The artist who could disentangle the subtle sound of an image from the mesh of its defining circumstances most exactly and "re-embody" in artistic circumstances chosen as the most exact for it in its new office, he was the supreme artist.

-James Joyce, *Stephen Hero*

Chapter 23

The lawyer, Jonny Quarrels, seduced Cindy at their first meeting, actually after they had dinner in an expensive downtown restaurant that was in the penthouse at the top of an office complex with a view of the Rocky Mountains. He had talked her into visiting his apartment for a drink.

He reminded her of an upscale version of Danny, who she would have to admit forever after still occupied a spot in her heart that was warm and well-lit, or at least warm and sticky, even though the son-of-a-bitch was still a son-of-a-bitch by definition and she still hoped he would rot in the lowest bowels of hell for all eternity. She gave up some time ago trying to reconcile her heart with her head; she had, after all, fallen in love with a murderer who was actively avoiding the law after she made love to him for three straight days, so this paradox was not so hard to live with. It was just so.

Sex with Jonny Quarrels was just so, too. Matter-of-fact. Just so-so, even. It did not last long and she dreamt of being with Zeke afterward, his body on top of her as warm and familiar as if she had known him for years instead of a few days.

Cindy had thought, even as the lawyer pushed his lawyer's tongue against her teeth the first time, that she might feel guilty the next day, but she didn't. She cared about Zeke, but he was gone, south like Zig, and maybe forever like him too. She had pretty much resigned herself to this migratory passage of men right through her life. Some, like Zig and Zeke, on a bullet train.

The larger reason she thought she might feel guilty, however, had to do with her long ago self-assignation to slut-dom. Her mother had told her over and over that good girls don't do this, that they marry the man who took their virginity, and then...

That was it. There had been no explanation after that, which made the part about virginity sound like an indictment at this stage in her life. But even if the first part came true, then what? Cindy wanted to know, now. For her mother it had been all pork chops and gravy and football on TV until her father died when Cindy was 13.

But there were other questions. What if that first one was damn disappointing? And what if he was dead? Zip, nada, nothing, like had been her mother's fate? What if they all passed through like 200 mph trains? Was she to blame, morally speaking, for that? These were all questions her mother had never raised, let alone answered, and Cindy felt a little stupid at the realization's late arrival.

Her only real regret after sex with Jonny Q. was that he was not Zeke, that Zeke was gone and, unlike Zig or anyone else, she wished he wasn't. That wish seemed irrational, not only because his absence was beyond her control, or because she had only known him a short time, too short a time to feel this way, but because the danger of his situation was dangerous for her too. She was, after all, the redhead on the news who was wanted for questioning about a double murder, plus a murder and a holdup. Life as math operation had suddenly flip-flopped, but addition seemed even worse than subtraction at this point. She was feeling overwhelmed and the realization in Jonny Quarrels' bed that she had so far been more worried about everything and anything than for her own possible troubles with the law made her feel neurotic.

The next morning she told Jonny Quarrels that he could take her to dinner one night a week if he wished, Saturday nights only, and that there would be no more screwing.

"You are in my employ, as it were, and such a relationship seems, well, unseemly," she told him. She knew he could appreciate the logic of her position, not to mention the word unseemly. It was one of those words rich people use consciously to delineate their class before the world, but it also left many of them open to manipulation by anyone who could imitate their diction and thereby infiltrate their ranks like a spy behind enemy lines.

For the lawyer's part, he told Cindy he loved her and would do whatever she wished. Aside from the fact that they had just met, and the fact that he was an attorney, the best criminal attorney in America perhaps but still an attorney, Cindy had no reason to doubt it. His resemblance to Danny aside. Lawyers, hell men in general, may be able to fake any emotion, but his fawning before the possibility of sex, however remote, could be used something like a cross between truth serum and a choke chain. Judging by Jonny Quarrels' energetic but strangely wan expression, as if his heart might break or he might howl at the moon for sheer joy, either one, she could trust him implicitly.

Chapter 24

That first night over dinner Cindy admitted to Jonny Q. who she was hiring his services to defend. She gave him an abbreviated account of the already, and inherently, abbreviated story of her relationship with Zeke after Jonny assured her that the client-lawyer relationship was sacrosanct, and after he went on at length about the constitutional guarantees, and precedence, and after he had offered oblique personal examples, many examples, where the courts had upheld that sanctity.

"Besides, if I can do some rudimentary investigation now, our case will be miles ahead when your...friend either comes in or is brought in."

Cindy had only told Jonny that she was with Zeke for three days. She didn't tell him how they had spent their time, so his uncertainty as to how to refer to Zeke in relationship to her was understandable. The slight hint of sarcasm she heard in his voice when he arrived at the word was Cindy's first clue the lawyer had more than a professional interest in her. That, and he seemed to visibly swoon, to flush and grab the edge of the table, when she told him how she earned her money. She thought at first that she had offended some puritan sensibility, but his grin when he regained control told her otherwise. His lascivious expression was her first recognition the lawyer reminded her of Danny, too.

"So," said Jonny Quarrels between the entree and dessert, "if you don't mind my asking, what exactly do you see in this man who is wanted for a double murder and who you have known for so short a time?"

It was a typical lawyer's ploy, the leap from "friend" to this question, but Cindy had half-expected him to ask it when she realized he was attracted to her. The truth was she did not really have an answer until that very moment when Jonny actually put it into words.

She had thought to say that the sex was extraordinary. It was the truth, although certainly flippant, and it would shut Jonny up, and off for that matter since she was having mixed emotions about his resemblance to Danny at this point.

She had thought to say that it was none of his fucking business, which was the truth too, more or less, but only more or less since this same lawyer might possibly have to defend her too and would need to know more about her relationship with Zeke.

She had thought to blame it all on fate, but the very concept frightened her. If she had no say in all these men's comings and goings, then where was she being led by all this frenetic addition and subtraction, and to what end? The absolute absence of control was too much to ponder.

So she told the truth as it came to her in an overpriced restaurant by candlelight while waiting for her flaming dessert to arrive.

"Zeke and I have something in common," she said. "We have both killed someone."

112

In spite of all the stories of mayhem and death Jonny Quarrels must have heard in his line of work, he was obviously taken aback by this news. He had been playing with a spoon and now dropped it on the table. His jaw dropped too, just as his spoon clanked against his water glass. A cartoon-like effect that nearly made Cindy laugh.

He leaned over the table and said in a low and shaking voice, "Something I will have to defend you for or have you been through the system already?"

"No. It's not like that," said Cindy. "I used to take pictures for a big photography studio, weddings mostly. Once, I took pictures at a ceremony in the mountains west of Boulder. It was beautiful. The bride was Catholic and the groom was Jewish so they combined elements of both religions rituals. Men in yarmulkes at a high mass. That kind of thing.

"Anyway, after all the posed stuff-groom's family, wife's family, bride stuffing groom with cake-I always liked to wander around and take pictures of everybody when they weren't looking. I have always fancied myself something of an artist, mostly an artist in search of a medium, but the truth is this limited spontaneity was as close to art as I could get in that job.

"So I'm clicking away at the reception when I see an old man asleep in a chair, his head resting peacefully on his chest, his hands folded in his lap. There is a young boy from the wedding party still in his tux sitting next to the old man and he's eating cake. The pictures I took of this little scene were pristine, beautiful, some of the best I had ever done.

"It turns out the old man is drunk and the kid is his grandson. The old man had apparently gotten drunk and passed out at every family gathering for twenty years, but not once had anyone ever confronted him. His family never said a word. He just snoozed in a corner somewhere and everybody pretended he didn't exist.

"Grandpa was also the bride's father, and she was the youngest of eight daughters. When all eight sisters saw my pictures, a bomb went off. He'd slept through each of their eight receptions.

"My pictures were the proverbial last straw. The sisters and their mother pooled their rage and assaulted the old man for every transgression, assailed him with twenty years of their collective feminine mortification, read him the familial riot act.

"Maybe he thought his drinking was a secret, or that it was acceptable since no one said anything before, or maybe he thought booze made him invisible since that's how everyone treated him. At any rate, rather than change his ways or defend himself or promise to change, this guy came to see me at my office.

"He tore at his hair and beat his chest and demanded I exonerate him. I'm not sure how he thought I could do that, but maybe it was my responsibility as the taker-of-the-fateful-picture, the producer of the tool that was his undoing, because I had the power of art at my disposal to contextualize him and thereby define him to the world.

"The next day I was fired for the disruption, and I was told that all my minor league attempts to make art of the mundane had yielded exactly this: a man wailing like an Old Testament prophet and spilling tears over my desk.

"The next day the old man hung himself in the family garage with his belt." Cindy drained her wine glass.

"I'm confused," said Jonny. "No judge in the world would deem this man's death the result of your action."

"Oh, but it was," said Cindy. "I was looking for a romantic symmetry in the world; it was, after all, a wedding, one of those vestigial remnants of our culture's naive belief in beauty and order and eternity. I projected a context onto that scene, the old guy asleep next to the kid eating cake, a context that did not exist, and does not exist in the modern world. Romantic symmetry is a lie, but I saw filial beauty as some diminished representative of that symmetry all-the-same when the S.O.B. was really comatose."

114

"I don't know about art," said Jonny Quarrels, "or about romantic symmetry. I'm not even sure what that means. But if there is one thing a lawyer knows it is how to engender or perpetuate or destroy any illusion, a talent we share in common with magicians and phone sex queens." Jonny Quarrels smiled like he meant this observation to be cute. Cindy clenched her fists and her knuckles grew white at the thought that she and the lawyer could share lying and manipulation as innate traits.

"An attorney gets his crack dealer client a G.I. haircut and dresses him in a Sears-Roebuck suit and asks his priest to testify about his troubled youth; an attorney asks a respected stockbroker, after he reminds him he is under oath before God, if he ever even once in his life dreamt of an under-aged girl without her clothes, which of course he has, although he may have never done more than dream; maybe an attorney finds witnesses to swear a wife-killer was a stressed but loving husband..."

"What's your point?" asked Cindy testily. Something in Jonny's last illustration made her even more angry. Mostly she had not tried to give any moral perspective at all to Zeke's murders, but merely accepted him because of how he made her feel. Jonny's example was threatening to make her think. "That reality is easily manipulated...?"

"That human beings see what there is to see, like you saw familial bliss in the old man and his grandson, within a particular context, projected or not. For you, that was the truth. An attorney gives a jury a context as well as the facts, which is how justice works in America, because that is the extent of human cognition."

The waiter set a bowl of flaming cherries before Cindy and a bowl before Jonny Quarrels. Their faces glowed across the table at each other like ritual masks.

"You merely saw that picture in a different context than the old man's daughters because you were not privy to their history."

"So I am an unwitting agent of fate," said Cindy flatly. "I take a picture and an old man dies and that's it. I have no responsibility, real or karmic, none?"

"I am a lawyer and so as a rule do not deal with the metaphysical. I'd explain this situation more as a complex cause and effect relationship; that which at first seemed so random merely turned out not to be because of factors beyond your knowledge. There was a reason the old man was asleep and it was his addiction."

"But aren't I guilty, however unwittingly, however accidentally, however tangentially, of this man's death? Isn't there some responsibility for the maker implicit in what was made and what it set in motion?"

"You're asking metaphysical questions again," said Jonny. "Culpability is a pretty straight forward cause and effect relationship for lawyers and judges, no matter how complex the actual events. It's part of a lawyer's job to make it simple, simplistic even, so the relationship is not beyond the limited capacity of the jurors to understand. You did not actually hang the old man, therefore you are not guilty."

Cindy ate her cherries in desultory silence as Jonny Quarrels made small talk about the law, how it worked and did not work.

"Art is dangerous," she told the waiter as he took her empty bowl. It was the only thing her conversation with Jonny had convinced her of.

Chapter 25

An old woman, with a face more wrinkled than any Cindy had ever seen, told her she had a stain on her spirit the size of a tundra sparrow. Cindy did not know if that was a large or small stain, spirit-wise, bird-wise for that matter.

The woman's name was Kalish, The Healer of Ketchikan, or so the ad said at the back of the New Age magazine Cindy had bought with her groceries a few days before. She had picked it up as she stood in line for something to look at, but decided to buy it when she saw the picture of an old woman with a 900 number under it. The old woman promised happiness, guaranteed it or your money back. She sat across from that woman now.

"Is that a big stain?"

"Depends on the size of the spirit," said Kalish. "Yours is fairly big, for one of your race, so the stain does not cover the whole spirit as it would with some people, most lawyers and politicians and corporate CEO's for example. But a stain is a stain and must be reckoned with."

Kalish never stopped smiling like an overly mysterious Tibetan Buddhist Cindy met once in Boulder, and as she smiled her eyes squinted together until they disappeared into the other folds of her face. Cindy was never quite sure if the old woman was looking at her or not. The Alaskan wind rattled the windows of the trailer house and whistled through some unseen crack in the wall.

"So what is this stain on my spirit and what exactly do you mean by reckon with?"

"You must tell me what the stain is, then we'll go from there."

"You mean you don't know what it is?"

"No. I know, but you must tell me."

Cindy had been sitting on the edge of the couch across from Kalish; now she sat back. "Well, there was this old man I took a picture of..."

"No," Kalish interrupted. "That isn't it, at least not the whole of it."

Cindy started to ask how she knew about the old guy and his suicide, but she didn't. Kalish had already proven to her that she knew things there was no feasible way she could know. It was why Cindy had flown to Alaska.

The old woman had told her much over the phone about her past that was true, about her mother and Danny and Zig, even about Zeke. Kalish hadn't used their names, of course, but what she said about all of them left little doubt in Cindy's mind who she was referring to, little doubt that the old lady knew things somehow.

Her reference to Zeke was as a fleeting shadow headed south with a piece of Cindy in his heart. Who else could it be? Zig was as far south, or any other direction, as he would get for years. Last she heard Danny was in Canada somewhere with his waitress-of-the-fishnet-stockings. Jonny Quarrels was in court defending some insurance executive against embezzlement charges. And that was the whole list of anyone who could possibly harbor any emotion toward her that could be interpreted as carrying a piece of her.

The old woman's words about all the people in Cindy's life were just as cryptic, and she recognized a quality in the language that resembled the fortune the gypsy palm readers at the county fair had given her every summer that she visited her grandmother. The gypsy's reading of her palm was always the same-always tall dark strangers and great wealth and many children-but then it was the same fortune the gypsy gave every young girl with a dollar.

Kalish's words seemed accurate enough however to get her on a plane. She thought if she talked to the woman face to face the answers to her questions would be more forthright. Kalish thought so too, something about a quality of the spirit phone wires could not carry, as long as Cindy brought 500 dollars with her.

So now she sat in Kalish's ancient trailer house on the edge of Ketchikan, Alaska as a warm wind off the ocean rocked the place. The woman's living room was filled with hundreds of whale figurines carved from ivory, driftwood, stone, and clay. There was even a blue stuffed pillow whale three feet long. Cindy looked around the room at the figures, while Kalish smiled and squinted, and pondered the tundra-sparrow-sized stain on her spirit.

She could think only in terms of the large questions: was the stain some sin she must expiate? Was it something she had failed to do? Was it emotional, some lack in herself? What did it have to do with the old man's suicide? Kalish did say it was not the whole of her stain, but that meant his death had something to do with it.

"Maybe I've screwed too many men," she heard herself say. The old woman laughed until she choked. Cindy had to slap her on the back to help her get her breath.

"I'm sorry," said Kalish when she got control of herself," but white people are so strange. All the things you could have said and out comes the puritan guilt thing, in your mother's very words probably."

"Probably," admitted Cindy, a little embarrassed at what she'd said and the reaction it provoked, "but why is that so funny?"

"Because you have no idea what you said, that is to say what it means. All this stuff is connected, your squeamishness about your sexuality and your relationship to men generally and to your mother and the old man's death, and it all points to something larger. It is so large, in fact, it's as if you carry a big blue whale around on your shoulders but you don't even know he's there. There is just a great weight."

The old woman was still smiling and squinting. She waved her hand around the room.

"All these whales represent my spirit animal, but also all those problems white people call me about."

"Are our problems merely all as big as whales, or are they the same big problem?" asked Cindy.

"Yes! Yes! I told you your spirit is big for one of your race," said Kalish and she clapped her hands like a trained seal claps its flippers, rhythmically, her arms outstretched.

"All my figures are whales, but some are wood and some stone and some ivory. The inflection changes, but the one big thing, the problem, is the same."

"You sound suspiciously like a pop-psychologist with a single simple answer for everybody."

This sent the old woman into another fit of laughter. Cindy slapped her on the back again, but not merely to help Kalish breath. She slapped her hard enough to transfer some of her annoyance at the old woman's outbursts at her expense.

"Oh my. You must forgive me once more Miss Sweet Stuff," said Kalish as she held her hand to her chest above her pendulous breasts, "but you are such a delight after all those others."

Kalish pointed to a frame that was on the wall above the couch and behind Cindy's head. Cindy had to stand to read it.

"A Ph.D. from Harvard," said Cindy flatly.

"Yes, class of "48.""

"So why all this masquerade if you're a shrink and not really some kind of healer?"

"Oh, but I am a healer Miss Sweet Stuff. I am the Healer of Ketchikan to tribals within hundreds of miles of this place. They just pay me in fish and seal meat instead of greenbacks. The degree is from my I-can-do-anything-a-white-person-can-do phase, not that some of that stuff doesn't come in handy sometimes, a small portion. My grandfather was a shaman up north, a man of great skill and power, and he passed a little of it to me the year I returned from Harvard, the year before he died."

"So is this whale some Jungian metaphor or is it tribal?" Cindy picked the whale pillow up and pointed it like a revolver at Kalish.

"The two are not mutually exclusive, but I was using it as my own metaphor, to make a point. Contrary to your assertion about my pop-psych simple answer, it isn't. Just like all those things, sex and men and the suicide, add up to one big problem you share in common with the rest of your race, reckoning with the stain on your spirit that is the sign of the problem is complicated. It involves not merely giving a name to the cure, which would be the same for all of you, but figuring out what that cure is specifically for Cindy Sweet Stuff."

"Maybe it's just all beyond me, like you seem to think it's beyond all white people generally," said Cindy. She had not slept in twenty-four hours in her haste to get here and to get answers and now the strain of Kalish's roundabout way of talking and her unsettling laughter were taking a toll.

"Oh, but you do know what that problem's name is, the cause of the stain. I can see what you know and what you don't, and this is not the heathen sage line I use to make my money. I can see that you know and you must bring what you know to the level of consciousness yourself, or the stain cannot be eradicated."

"If the heathen New Age entrepreneur isn't talking now, who is?" asked Cindy. The doctor or the shamaness?"

Kalish stood and walked to the front door. She laid her hand on the knob.

"Remember the reason you're here. You want happiness. Think about every man you have known and what you expected of him. Think about the suicide and your role in it and why you blame yourself. Figure out the correlation, Cindy Sweet Stuff.

"Now give me your money and go home. Call me when you have an answer, and I will help you reckon with your tundra-sparrow-sized stain. Free-of-charge, of course."

Interlude

Zeke fell asleep as the Buick cruised over the desert like a mirage. The cool pines had given way to sagebrush and mesquite and scrub cedar, which gave way to barrel cactus and saguaro and low growing desert plants Zeke did not know the names of. Heat waves shimmered from the road, from the Earth. Zeke fell asleep with Beak's words rowing through his mind like ravens row through the air: malaise, purpose...malaise, purpose...

In his dream a large black bird flew southward, over the rim of the world. The bird carried Marianne's head in its beak by her hair.

121

Blood dripped from her neck to the ground miles below, and left a trail, a stain on the sand.

Marianne was whistling, contrapuntally, the saddest music Zeke had ever heard. A requiem. Each note carried sadness on its back, like the coyote had carried sadness on his back, as dark and dangerous and necessary gifts.

In his dream Zeke felt the first tender blades of remorse slice through him. In his dream Zeke said, over and over, I am sorry. But Marianne only whistled as the great bird flew inevitably south, as oblivious of him in death as she had been in life.

Part Four

It is a bitter truth our voyages teach! Tiny and monotonous,
the world has shown-will always show us-what we are: oases of
fear in the wasteland of ennui!
                    -Charles Baudelaire, *Les Fleurs du Mal*

Chapter 26

On his trip south with Francis, Zeke had been awakened by the heat. The temperature was only in the mid-80's, but after the cold of Denver and the cool of the high desert Zeke was sweating and uncomfortable against the Buick's plastic covered seats.

When Zeke woke up Francis told him they were nearly to May's whorehouse. The car rolled through low-rent housing projects that stood row on row as far as the eye could see, rolled to the very southern edge of Phoenix. The cheap three story buildings gave way to much older clapboard houses and run-down businesses: tattoo parlors, peep shows, used car dealers.

May's stood at the end of all this squalor, on the verge of pure desert. It was a Victorian style house painted bright yellow with a sign above the door that said, "May's Boarding House."

Zeke wondered only briefly how Francis knew the way so well, since many a side street had to be negotiated to get here. Francis threw the wooden screen door open and walked in as if he were home. He hugged each woman in turn and introduced them to Zeke. There were four Marias, numbered by size or age, Zeke could not tell which; Marie number one was petite and very young, through Maria four who was very large and forty-ish. There were two Consuelas, a Candy and an Eloise. All were dressed in thin night gowns awaiting customers in the front foyer of the house. All cooled themselves with heart-shaped oriental fans.

Then May had shown up. Without a word she picked Francis up by his lapels and threw him through the still open door. Francis landed on the porch and rolled down the three steps to the sidewalk. When she turned to grab Zeke he held up his hands and tried to explain that he was looking for a friend, Bob Chance. May flew into a rage at the mention of Chance's name. She screamed at him in Spanish and stomped out of the room. Zeke could have sworn the floor shook under her.

One of the Consuelas, in her early thirties with a beer belly as opposed to the other Consuela who was built like a child and not more than fifteen, interpreted: Miss May says the lazy son-of-a-bitch is next door, at Miguel's Tavern.

Zeke shook his hand and wished him good luck as Francis rubbed the back of his head where his body had first made contact with the porch, as he looked sidelong at the front door to the bordello as if May would burst through it any minute, looking for him. Zeke entered the bar next door to May's bordello as the Buick's tires squealed. He had left his only possessions, the coat Cindy had given to him and Cantarita's sleeping bag, on May's front porch under a bench. He thought of both women as he stuffed his gear there, how they seemed to have been in his life a lifetime ago. He was depressed for exactly seven seconds, but the nature of reality and time were beyond him, and for the first time in many days he told himself, I ain't no Einstein. The depression disappeared in an instant as if the assertion were a magic spell.

It was late afternoon, but the sun seemed hotter and brighter than when he woke up in the Buick. The air conditioned darkness behind the heavy wooden door of the bar wrapped around him like arms, soothed him, and Zeke nearly sighed as he stood just inside the door feeling the sweat evaporate from his skin and letting his eyes adjust. Zeke knew Chance was there and where he was in the room even before he could see. He heard the endless rumble of his voice.

"God is a singular chaos, all encompassing, mind-exploding chaos; or if God is an overarching order, it is order on a scale that is beyond our human capacity to understand. God is a super-fractal, maybe.

"Either way, the trouble for us is that the context is just too damned big. We have done the best we can with our bicameral brain: here/absent, true/false, alive/dead, clarity/ confusion, right/wrong...but such a list is endless and ultimately limited, paradoxically, since no entry can be mutually exclusive in order to define nuance. Alive contrasts with dead but also comatose; clarity contrasts with confusion, but both contrast with transcendent wisdom, whatever the hell that might be...

"It is impossible to define the world let alone God via such a hodge-podge of theses and antitheses. Even if we could stand the mess of such a method, we are obviously mortal and we just plain run out of time."

Chance leaned heavily at the bar, knocking over two of the empty brown beer bottles from the line in front of him. A small, completely bald man sat to his right on a tall, green vinyl stool with aluminum legs.

The small, bald man to Chance's right interrupted him, slurring his words slightly. "God must be order. I cannot live any other way. I look up at the Mexican sky at night when I am in the field, at the literally endless expanse of the stars, and I know all that I have lived through, even when I have suffered, must mean something."

"Why, because you exist?" said Chance, a hint of ridicule in his voice. "That's a very circular argument, not to mention strongly homocentrist, for a supposed man-of-science." Chance held up two fingers to the bartender, a thin and frail-looking Hispanic with a long mustache.

"Some men look at those same stars and know that humans mean absolutely nada," said Chance. "That in the face of eternity we aren't even a blink and that all human action breeds nothing of much import to anyone but the actor, if indeed him."

"You're a fucking atheist of the worst stripe, Bob Chance," said his companion.

"On the contrary. I am an unwilling agnostic maybe, but a skeptic who actually envies your belief in humanly perceivable order. I am an endless searcher for purpose, anyway, orders most obvious human counterpart." Chance held his hand to his heart in a grandiose gesture of piety.

Zeke remembered Beak's words, his admonition that he must find a purpose, but also his assertion that death and life were the same meaningless malaise for Zeke's race, and he grew uneasy. He could not even find the will to summon his mantra. I ain't no Einstein, indeed.

He walked to the bar and tapped Chance's shoulder. Chance turned, bleary eyed, surprised, and hugged him like a long lost brother, even though it had only been a few days since he had dropped Zeke and Cantarita at her brother's in Tuba City. Chance introduced his companion as Strauss, a cultural anthropologist.

"Really a cultural voyeur," said Chance. "Strauss records a tribe's music and stories ostensibly for interpretation and posterity, but really he is trapping the culture in a machine.

"Hell, I heard what sounded like Navajo drum and flute music on the radio the other day, but it had been generated by a computer hooked to a synthesizer, programmed mechanical randomness. There was an interview with the guy who claimed responsibility, some Hungarian. He was damn proud of himself. Probably used your work from north of here a few years ago to rip off the Indians, Strauss."

Chance laughed derisively and took a long swallow from his beer bottle.

Strauss, who had stood and saluted Zeke drunkenly when introduced, became sullen. He ordered a shot of tequila and peeled the label from one of the many empties before him on the bar with his thumbnail.

Chance asked Zeke about Cantarita and told him he was sorry, like Zeke had said she died, when he heard they were no longer together.

"What a shame for you," he said and ordered Zeke a beer. "There is something special about that woman, aside from her unbelievably primal beauty, I mean. Something that can't be seen,

128

that maybe doesn't have a name, but that seems quintessentially human, a kind of raw intelligence and enthusiasm that I thought had been bred out of the species by now, here at the sad dawn of the 21st century. It is heartening really, to think there is at least one person left filled to the brim with human potential."

"Purpose," said Strauss without lifting his eyes from the half-peeled label of the beer bottle. "You were talking about purpose, you monstrous asshole."

"Of course. Maybe what I sense in Cantarita is some kind of ambient purpose that she herself has yet to discover."

Chance raised his beer bottle in salute. "To Cantarita's discovery of her purpose," he said, and took a long swallow.

The black storm of Zeke's depression rose again fully formed. He thought about what Beak had said, about Zeke and Cantarita both being on the reservation for a purpose, but the only reason for Zeke's appearance there seemed to be a growing sense of shame for his failure to feel anything like remorse, let alone to understand his murder of Marianne and the plumber, for his race's service to death as Beak called it.

He had a growing sense that he carried the weight of the malaise of his species on his back, Zeke Reilly the culmination of Western Civilization's loss of a reason for being, his body was some kind of marker, an empty symbol, a husk only that reeked of his race's despair like a corpse.

"It is what we lack as a species," said Chance, as if reading his mind, "Noble, ennobling, purpose."

Chance pulled a small plastic bag from his shirt pocket, poured several tiny white pills into his hand, and chased them down his throat with beer. He shook his head and shuddered. He made exaggerated noises like a horse blowing air from its nostrils.

"I don't give the species much in the way of odds, to tell you the truth...when it comes to survival, I mean," he said. "Especially with the advent of global capitalism.

"Capitalism is its own reason for being, a feedback loop within which the individual produces to consume, and that is supposed to be enough to keep us satisfied. It is supposed to equal purpose."

Chance was talking faster and faster now, and Zeke marveled that the amphetamines could enter his blood stream so fast.

"Hell, here in the U.S.A. we don't even produce anything anymore. We've added a step to the process and become a nation of middlemen. We just sell shit to each other. Like Miller's pathetic salesman, we don't put a nut to a bolt, we don't grow anything but the illusion of prosperity and health and joy, the illusion that gets us converts worldwide, converts who will make the shit we sell to each other in the hope of getting in on the illusion too, the big capitalist hallucination.

"And that shit we sell each other is now made in Malaysia by children chained to machines, by prisoners in China, by immigrants to this country who fled crazy fuckers who seem to want to kill everybody in Central and South America only to find the promised land is a buck-an-hour-twelve-hours-a-day in a sweatshop hidden somewhere in the ghettos of L.A."

The speed of Chance's delivery wasn't the only thing picking up. His pitch and volume were rising too, and Zeke began to feel self conscious. He didn't dare to look around, but he felt eyes upon their little group. He put a hand on Chance's forearm, hoping to get his attention, to signal him inconspicuously to lower the noise level of this harangue, but Chance threw his arms upward at the same moment to gesticulate a wild accompaniment to his sermon and inadvertently threw Zeke's hand off without even noticing he had been touched.

"Consumption, or the possibility for consumption, is supposed to be enough to keep us all breathing, but you can feel the whole goddamn mess simmering just under a full goddamn boil on every goddamn metropolitan street in goddamn America." Chance slammed his beer bottle down on the bar sloshing foam out the top.

He was rolling now, like an evangelical preacher at full throttle. Zeke pushed his chin to his chest and looked at the small piece of pocked bar in front of him, trying to be invisible, hoping no one looking their direction at the commotion would recognize the double murderer from his picture on the tube.

He doubted that in postmodern America, where mayhem was just part of the day's entertainment mix, anything short of all out mass murder was news a thousand miles away from the event, but what if someone in the bar had been in Denver at the time, been visiting relatives or holed up in a Motel-Six with a lover, had seen the reward flashed across the screen?

"So what about you?" asked Strauss. I hear a whole lot of bombastic, Marxist-sounding bullshit out of you, but what is purpose for you?"

Chance stood ceremoniously and raised the shot of whiskey the skinny Hispanic bartender with the Pancho Villa mustache just set in front of him.

"The untold want by life and land never granted,/ Now voyager sail thou forth to seek and find," said Chance nearly at the top of his lungs.

"Don't give me that abstract crap. I mean you, Bob-goddamn-Chance," Strauss yelled before Chance could chase his recitation with the contents of his glass. Strauss pointed his index finger at Chance as if aiming a gun at him and squinted. He pitched dangerously from side to side on his stool.

"No hypothetical everybody you, but you, Bob-double-goddamn-Chance."

"Like the poet said, life is a voyage of discovery."

"Bullshit," Strauss bellowed louder even than Chance at his most vociferously evangelical, still pointing, still squinting. "The voyage implies both a destination and a return trip home and you have neither destination or home. Besides, the poet believed in heroes, the voyager as hero, and that sure as hell is not you."

131

Chance was quiet for a moment, his glass still suspended in the air. He looked at Strauss as if surprised by the zealousness of the attack, as if appraising what he had just heard.

Zeke still did not dare to look around the room, but now he was certain all eyes in the bar were on them. There was no sound, neither conversation or the clink of glass. The whole bar waited to hear what Chance would say.

Chance threw back his shot and slammed the glass to the bar. He wiped his mouth on the back of his hand.

"Well Strauss, I'm doing this minimalist, Zennist, reductionist thing now. I've boiled life down to its core constituents: fucking, eating, drinking copious quantities of booze..."

"Ah, so life's core constituents include self-administered anesthesia?" Strauss tried to pronounce the last word three times before he gave up.

"Damn right," said Chance. "A man does not get to be my age in this debauched age without a pile of regrets so big it threatens to swallow him."

"Explain," said Strauss, though it came out S-plain.

Chance ordered himself and Zeke another beer, but ran his finger across his throat and pointed at Strauss as a sign the bartender should serve no more alcohol to the anthropologist. Strauss watched the gesture but either did not understand it or did not care.

"Well, I'm guilty of things I did not mean to be guilty of," said Chance. "They just happened. In spite of my best efforts and intentions. For example, during my stint in academia I merely helped turn out future buyers and sellers, middlemen and women."

"So what," stammered Strauss. "You failed as a teacher..."

"Worse than that," said Chance. "We all failed. Some few of my colleagues were also swimming upstream against the status quo, and they ended up broken and sad and suicidal, nearly mad with what they, we, came to know with perfect certainty: that it is too late.

"The race is in thrall now, completely, to the forces of control via mass and popular culture. All our students will ever live for is to watch TV and to make some money, no matter what one or two of their teachers say or do."

"So by definition, purpose cannot help but equal hedonism in a debauched age?" asked Strauss. Zeke heard a sneer in his voice now, anger.

"It isn't that simple, Strauss. There are other complications that make anesthesia, as you call it, necessary. The accumulated weight of memory plus our inevitable mortal fear plus powerlessness equals...I don't know...this," Chance said as he swung his arm wide to indicate the bar, or maybe the world, Zeke was not certain.

"There are ex-wives who have fucked ex-friends and destroyed gardens where petunias and pumpkins and corn and beans once flourished as in Eden. There are prostate problems and ulcers and chronic shoulder pain that indicate the ride is at least half-over. There are all those young faces, so wistful and generous and beautiful, all stupid as cows...."

"Bob Chance's list of reasons to get shit-faced," said Strauss sarcastically.

"Yeah, but in spite of it all I have hope, Strauss."

"Hope! You can't use that word, you godless bastard!" Strauss slammed his fist on the bar and knocked over the empties that remained. Chance steadied him with one arm to keep him from falling off of his stool.

Zeke looked up the bar nervously. The bartender was wiping the bar and watching them from the corners of his eyes. Two large Hispanic men in identical black t-shirts and with identical goatees who were seated at the bar watched them, too, identical sunglasses pushed to the front of their heads just above the hairline.

"Hope is not an atheist's word," shouted Strauss.

"I told you I am an unwilling agnostic. Maybe what separates me from the atheist is precisely hope, that eventually I can turn

133

upward from this nihilist agenda toward the air and light of a transcendentally moral intent, that life will matter...in spite of all this bullshit," said Chance, and again he waved his arm in front of him to encompass the room or the world, "Hope still breathes in me. I catch a faint whisper of it doing just that sometimes...breathing, softly."

"Pig shit Hungarians might steal my work to betray the people whose way of life I am struggling to help them regain," said Strauss, spit flying from his mouth and over the bar, "but you are a romantic and that is a paradox I simply cannot abide: a romantic goddamn atheist. Hope!? We realists struggle through the world without it!"

Chance laughed. "You defined your existence a little while ago in relationship to the night sky, you are trying to help some Indians down in Mexico go backward in time toward some aesthetic of noble savagery, and you call me a romantic?"

Strauss swung a big, drunken roundhouse right at Chance's head, but he missed and fell off his stool. His face hit the floor with a *thunk* like dropped raw pot roast. Blood spurted from Strauss' nose and ran down his shirt and spotted the floor as Zeke helped him to his feet.

Chance pointed at the anthropologist and hollered loud enough, Zeke was certain, to be heard at May's: "The death of hope signals a massive failure of the will, because hope is the last lonely agent of the will, Strauss!"

Zeke guided the anthropologist toward the door by his arm. He wanted to separate the two men, but he also knew Strauss needed air badly. His eyes were crossed and his color was gone. But Zeke also wanted to get away from the conversation himself. He was almost grateful Strauss had swung at Chance.

A wave of déjà vu swept over him when he and Strauss were halfway to the door. He had to half-haul Strauss now, whose body seemed to want desperately to yield to gravity, to go down in a heap. Zeke's eyes darted back and forth instinctively, trying to

134

decipher the scene, to put circumstances to his own growing disequilibrium. Then he saw them.

There were four men at a table in the darkened corner nearest the door. He noticed them because he'd seen them in a dream, but also because they looked so out of place. The other bar patrons were poor, working men and women, or unemployed men and women perhaps, but all in jeans or shorts and t-shirts. These four were in suits with creases as sharp as knives, their ties loosened, their shoes black and shiny even in the low light of the bar. One of the men wore aviator's sunglasses, like only pilots and policemen wear.

Zeke looked away quickly and tried to put Strauss' wilting and blood-stained body between himself and their corner table.

Chance raged on even as they reached the door, as Zeke pushed it open and pulled Strauss through it, as the door closed slowly behind them. Zeke could see Chance, still at the bar, framed in the doorway, legs spread and finger pointed at them like a weapon: "Many a loved one has disappeared from someone's life, or died, or worse...," he shouted, "because a man failed to protect them with hope, because he could no longer envision the good or the beautiful even for those most dear to him..."

Chance's voice disappeared as the door closed tightly, as Zeke and Strauss moved up the street toward May's in the blinding sunlight and through the heavy waves of heat.

****

F.B.I. agents kicked in May's front door the next morning. In full swat gear they searched every room, scaring every woman and her customer, even scaring May herself, or so she said as she told the story, until they found Chance in bed with the older Consuela. They hauled him away in handcuffs as Zeke and Strauss slept in Strauss' camper in the desert behind May's Boarding House.

135

May had sent the youngest Maria with the news, and Strauss and Zeke stumbled to the house for more information, aspirin, and a blood red concoction that smelled flammable and that Strauss chugged down without stopping. He immediately puked, then sweated for thirty minutes, pronounced himself cured, and went in search of Miguel the bartender.

Zeke was asleep in the kitchen, his head resting on the table, when Strauss returned a few hours later with a newspaper. Walt Whitman, Chance's Labrador, sulked in the corner.

According to Miguel, said Strauss, Chance turned his finger-like-a-gun on the four men in suits in the corner right after he and Zeke left. Chance had hollered that he could smell they were DEA and accused them of coming to Mexican Town to bust young brown men, to send them to jail to keep them from reproducing like they had been doing to young black men for years.

"It's something Chance has been raging about forever," Strauss said, as May poured the three of them the strongest coffee Zeke had ever tasted. "He's been saying the war on drugs is hegemonic since I met him, that the government uses it as an excuse to purify the race, but that drugs are also...and this part, the paradox, I never quite understood...the only way for poor people to get a chunk of the American Dream. I think he saw it as both carrot and stick, but also chains, as in addiction, the limitations of living so far outside the mainstream. As usual the idea makes some sense, but Chance managed to put a spin on it that hinted of paranoia.

"Anyway, Miguel said he was just about to have these two 300 pound guys he lets drink for free for protection, the Jimenez twins, escort Chance to May's, when the twins apparently tuned into what Chance was saying and headed toward the guys at the corner table.

"Miguel says he told them to back off, but I guess Chance had awakened the Jimenez brothers' racial indignation and they proceeded to beat the shit out of the DEA agents."

136

May launched into machine-gun Spanish as she poured them all another cup of coffee. Zeke only caught the dirty words, mother fuckers and cocksuckers and the like, because May said these in English. Strauss smiled at her and patted her big hand when she sat down.

"Chance would have been OK if he had left then, while the Jimenez brothers were dismantling those guys, but Miguel said he just kept hollering about how the poor were kept too busy with drugs and the drug trade and the law to get radicalized, stuff he's said to me a thousand times before.

"Even all this might not have been enough to get him taken away in chains, but then he launched into a diatribe I haven't heard before. The twins apparently had the agents boxed into a corner and were randomly punching them in the face too fast for any of them to pull out a gun, and Chance started hollering about anarchy as the only hope for human salvation, that human beings could only be free and equal in the confusion between regimes."

Strauss grew quiet for a few minutes, held his coffee cup in both hands, and stared into the miniscule steam as it was overwhelmed by the Arizona heat dried air, as it disappeared an inch above the rim. It was May's turn to comfort him and she patted him on the arm and made soothing noises in Spanish. Zeke heard *verdad* and *sufrimiento* and *desorden*: truth, suffering, trouble.

"Then he really stepped in it," said Strauss. "He told the agents that the only rich man who could empathize with the people would be one with stumps, that the only good president America would ever have would be one who had stared into the open space where his hands used to be after a bomb removed them. That's what they arrested him for," he said and pushed the paper across the table to Zeke.

The headlines said, "Transient Arrested for Threats Against the President."

137

"It seems the president of the U.S.A. is due in Phoenix in a few days," said Strauss and he laughed. "Irony always was Chance's forte, but this time the cosmic variety seems to have bit him in the ass."

****

The newspaper account speculated that Chance was possibly linked to the unabomber, or was at least part of a larger conspiracy of disaffected former academics who felt disenfranchised from the American mainstream, "possibly because they had been denied tenure."

This amused Strauss no-end and he laughed until he cried, and then he just cried. May held him, his head to her large bosom, until his grief passed.

"Sorry," he said to Zeke as May patted his bald head and left the kitchen to greet a customer in the foyer. He wiped his nose on his sleeve and stood to follow May.

"Chance told me once that the old Oscar Meyer Wiener song was not only an example of extreme commodity fetishism in which the singer longs to become a meat by-product, but emblematic of our nihilism since the singer also longs to be devoured." Strauss chuckled and wiped fresh tears from his eyes. Then he sang the song. "...then there will be nothing left of me," it ended in off-key tenor.

"To be certain, I told him, it is a damn strange sentiment, but that it was a sign of the culture's perverse desire to disappear seemed a stretch, at the time...the son-of-a-bitch may be too smart for his own good." He took his cup to the sink.

"I'm afraid our friend has become a participant-observer in the machinations of official power, and that he will be one for some time to come. These guys don't play, and they've got all the juice in this situation. Our so-called civil rights don't exist, in other words. I read about a guy once who was arrested for this same kind of

138

thing, threats against the president. Bush, I think. He was never convicted, but he was locked up in Wyoming, or some such place, for over a year getting psychologically probed, then another year or so just getting tried before they found him innocent and let him go, and I doubt the poor bastard had Chance's propensity for flaming oratory. Chance's mouth will get him life somewhere, one kind of jail or another-prison or bedlam..."

Strauss wandered out of the kitchen, to find May, to get some comfort, he said. The dog followed him.

Zeke poured the last of the coffee into his cup and opened the paper. The giant type of a full page ad made his heart beat like a big bass drum: WOMAN WITH NO IMAGINATION SEEKS MAN WHO AIN'T NO EINSTEIN FOR LOVE AND SNICKERDOODLES.

There was a 900 number at the bottom of the page.

Interlude

Zeke lay awake in Strauss' camper running through the fiercely apocalyptic words and events of the last several days. Strauss had some bureaucratic maneuvering to do in Phoenix, something to do with his grant, and said they could leave for Mexico in a few days. He told Zeke if he straightened things out with the granting agency he would take him along as his field research assistant. There was money in the budget and his previous assistant, a grad student from Illinois, had quit unexpectedly, for reasons Strauss was vague about; but there were hints the young man quit because there were dangers in the mountains he could not abide.

In the meantime they had moved Strauss' rig, a large cab-over camper atop a dual wheeled Ford pickup, further into the desert behind the brothel to get some distance from Chance's last known address. Strauss said he had enough problems with his grant

139

without publicity, and Zeke merely went along under the auspices of being Strauss' future, at least potential, anthropological assistant.

May's Boarding House was now a dot of light amid many dots of light along the horizon. At this distance they looked to Zeke, as he stared out the window above the cab of the truck where his bunk was, like fallen stars. There were thousands of stars above the horizon, distant and cold, or so they seemed in spite of the heat of the desert which was still considerable even though the sun had been down for hours and the real heat of summer was only a persistent rumor. Zeke imagined the lights of Phoenix as outcasts from the sky.

He pondered chaos and order and the entropy of late civilization until his head hurt. He was tempted to say it, I ain't no Einstein, but he didn't. He doubted if anyone, Beak and Chance included, could really understand this era and its discontents. So how could he?

But Beak's words weighed heaviest, the ones specifically about Zeke himself, and one word weighed more than all the rest combined, its specific gravity maybe the same as the weight of the language itself. Purpose.

Zeke was certainly on a journey, a voyage, like Chance had talked about, like his quote from Whitman; but, just as Strauss had said to Chance in the bar, destination and a return trip were beyond comprehension. He began to believe as he stared at the stars that his voyage was to hell. He would go south, the direction circumstances were pushing him whether he wanted to go or not, until he fell off the end of the world into a sea of flame and burn for eternity in answer for his lack of comprehension, his apathy, his stupidity. He would burn not only for Marianne and the plumber, but because he lacked a reason for his very existence. Hell, he seemed to lack affect entirely. He was just here, merely here and being pushed elsewhere.

The day before, Zeke had been nearly overwhelmed by what he had done in Denver, not so much the actual murders, which was the point, but his lack of conscience and, especially, the slow leaking from memory even of the blood he had spilled. He had felt the partial birth of remorse in his dream in Francis' Buick, but now he could barely see Marianne's face with its red third eye in his mind, no matter how hard he tried. He had meant to stare into her dead aspect in his imagination until he felt the full weight of his guilt descend in the hope that he might be utterly consumed now and not have to be pushed toward whatever terrible fate awaited him further south, but at best he could only recall her scrawny body. The face remained distorted, scrambled like they do on TV to hide someone's identity.

Then he remembered his conversation with Chance that first night at the Motel Zanzibar while Cantarita slept. He remembered how Chance wished aloud that he had killed his ex-wife, and Zeke needed an answer. Perhaps Chance would tell him there was some primal urge that was beyond comprehension, that explained Zeke's behavior and response, some vestigial impulse to destroy what you can't have and that cannot be logically explained or excised or avoided. If anyone knew of such a mechanism in the human psyche, he was certain it would be Chance. This was a last opportunity to rationalize what he had done.

So, he had asked the older Consuela to visit Chance in jail and to ask the question for him, though he was fairly certain the question itself, why Zeke wanted to know, would be a riddle to Chance. Consuela had banged on the camper door a few hours before, and the answer she delivered left Zeke more desperately empty than ever.

"Señor Chance says..." And here Consuela cast her eyes upward and her voice sounded as if she was reciting from a script. "The bitch had a black belt in cruelty and used it on him often, but he says it is not up to him who is to live and who is to die. He says that would be the negation of hope, to make himself the absolute center of the world and to judge all behavior by that standard." Consuela stopped for a moment, trying to read Zeke's expression.

141

Perhaps seeing Zeke's confusion, she said, "I reminded Señor Chance that you only have to walk down the streets to the west of here to believe in hell, what with drug dealers and gunshots every night. The wicked must suffer mightily." Then she crossed herself and kissed the crucifix that hung around her neck and left for May's, cutting through the cholla and soap weed in the dark. Zeke had nearly choked.

Now, in the desert night, he tried once more to recall Marianne to his mind's eye, to attempt penance, but her mother's beautifully genteel face floated before him instead, angelic and happy, then Judy's face became Cindy's. Zeke fell into sleep and dreamt of her soft and freckled flesh, of her small perfect breasts, of the multivariate tones of her in ecstasy, and the weight fell away again.

Whether this dream was memory or prescience, however, Zeke could not tell.

****

"Awareness is a great freedom and a great burden. Most of those around you are the walking dead, slaves to the way things are. You, on the other hand, are free, with all that entails, and you can't pretend not to be, can't pretend you're like those others."

Although they were talking on the phone, separated by many thousands of miles, Cindy was certain the old woman was smiling and squinting, a pile of happy wrinkles atop a square frame.

Cindy had worked the problem the old woman had set for her somewhat backward, at least obliquely. She had thought to simplify it by boiling the constituents down to a common factor. What do the men in your life, your mother, the old man's suicide, etc. have to do with your happiness, the old woman had asked? Cindy had merely rephrased the question: since the object of her journey to Ketchikan had been to find happiness, what did these things have to do with her visit with Kalish?

142

Cindy was convinced the answer lay hidden somewhere in the cryptic remarks the old woman made that day. In fact, it turned out Kalish had given her pretty obvious hints during their face-to-face chat. You know, she had said at one point, but you don't know that you know. More mystical bullshit packaged for the gullible, Cindy thought, but maybe there was some truth to be discovered through this game the old woman was playing, whether Kalish intended it or not.

So Cindy dialed Kalish's 900 number and said simply, "Awareness," when the old woman said hello. Although Cindy still wasn't sure what the connection was between Zeke and Zig and Danny et al. and her mother and the old man, and etc., and her happiness, awareness must mean something, she thought. At least it was a word Danny used a lot in his mysterious East phase. The old woman seemed delighted with her answer at any rate, and Cindy hoped to learn more by appearing to understand more than she actually did.

"But awareness is only the first step," said Kalish after giggling like a girl and complimenting Cindy once more on her difference from the rest of her race.

"To be certain, whites generally stumble the whole way from birth to death without understanding much of anything in large part because they don't notice anything, but just noticing is not enough. You must learn to live with both flux and paradox, and to act in spite of it all."

There was a moment of silence. Whether Kalish expected some reply from her or was organizing her thoughts, Cindy could not tell. She didn't want to reveal to the old woman how little she had really figured out, however, so she decided to wait her out.

After a few long minutes the old woman clicked her tongue and giggled.

"It is a paradox, for example," she continued, "that the world is complete as it is, that it's beautiful even, but humans are

143

inherently creatures of insatiable desire and desire is the antithesis of acceptance...so they can't even accept perfection.

"In fact desire suggests the possibility of some final fulfillment. Desire is the very engine of change, so you, Cindy Sweet Stuff, have no choice, in spite of the absurdity of the whole proposition, but to change the world and your life: daily and endlessly and incrementally, slowly or in big bites..."

"But this is all abstract bullshit," interrupted Cindy. Anything even remotely mystical sounding gave her a stomach ache ever since Danny went through a Zen-phase early in their marriage and continually spouted conundrum like he knew what it meant.

"I'll tell you a secret," said Kalish. "Every day is the eve of the apocalypse. Since the first creature achieved the first rudimentary self-awareness we have been staving off chaos, which is another word for inevitability, for death. Everything is rotting around us, falling down, falling to pieces, but we can imagine a different perfection than this one of decay, of florescence and rot. We can imagine its obverse, uninterrupted creation, and so we struggle toward some ideal. It is the essence of human action, though as I said most whites don't know it, but you have to figure out what you, Cindy Sweet Stuff, will do."

"You're an annoying old woman," said Cindy. She felt like vomiting. "You expect me to believe this crap about perfection when you live in a dented tin can with your Harvard Ph.D. on the wall and rip off unsuspecting white people? Is that perfect action for Kalish, The Healer of Ketchikan?"

"Yes," said Kalish flatly, "although I'd argue that I don't steal anything from them. I give all my patients something they hunger for, wisdom, albeit far less romantic tribal fare, and far more useful, than most whites expect or understand.

"Now quit wasting both our precious time," she said, and Cindy thought she heard a hint of anger in her voice. "You're an artist and you have some financial resources and the world is rotting." Kalish hung up.

144

Cindy got an Alka-Seltzer and pondered the old woman's new riddle. What did she mean, Cindy was an artist? She talked dirty for money and taught other women how to do the same. She was only an amateur photographer. What the hell did the old woman expect her to do? Talk creative trash to people as she took their picture?

Cindy fell asleep on the couch, more confused by this conversation with Kalish than she was before her clever answer, "awareness." She dreamt of Zeke. He held her somewhere in the desert and their sweat ran together in rivulets to the sand, but his hands and his breath were cool as water, his touch the pure cold of spring snow. In her dream she smiled at the sappiness of the image and its attendant metaphor, she smiled in her sleep on her actual couch in Colorado.

The next morning she would take out a full page ad in every newspaper between here and the Mexican border, and maybe a few on the other side. The old woman was at least right about one thing: Cindy had the means now to act, to change her life. This might not be the step she needed to take to fulfill her destiny, or whatever it was Kalish was provoking her to do, but it was a step and she wanted more than anything to see Zeke again. She hoped he felt the same.

Part Five

Perhaps, maybe, we'll see how the world ends.
-Alonzo Gonzalez Mó

Here, in the realm of decline, among momentary days, be the crystal cup that shattered even as it rang.
-Rilke, *Sonnets to Orpheus, II, 13*

Chapter 27

The further south he traveled, Zeke decided, the more bizarre, other worldly even, the melodrama that passed for his life became. In spite of his tendency to versions of consciousness most people did not suffer, normal people he thought bitterly, probably because of those experiences, he found the universe growing stranger by the minute. He considered the possibility that this was madness, that he was losing his mind by increments that had something to do with the direction he traveled, but could not convince himself. After all, Beak shared like experiences and, from the sound of it, much that was stranger than Zeke could even imagine, and yet he seemed sane within the context of his tribal beliefs, however weird Zeke might think his self-appointed task to save the world from evil.

Ultimately, he tried to take comfort in the small realization that, however increasingly odd the circumstances around him, people remained the same: some few were benevolent like Cantarita and her preacher; some outright evil, and he had to admit that this designation was becoming increasingly blurred, becoming a larger and larger category in his imagination based on his own possible assignation to it and Beak's adamant pronouncements about his race generally; but most people were innocuous zombies rolling with the pitch and heave of existence as if there were no pitch and heave. He had seen these last all along his route, from waitresses to road workers to truck drivers to the wealthy Mexican businessman Strauss had helped to change a tire just over the border: all ignorantly happy in the mundane world, all without a clue the world around them was chaos itself, at best a circus complete with clowns like himself and acrobats like Beak and Cantarita's mother straddling a growing abyss.

149

But then there was Cindy, her outright joy in his company regardless of his tendency to foreboding and depressive silences, her physical presence that was pure sex on legs, her peculiar intelligence that made him think of Judy but more powerful, more restless, like a boiling volcano but with a hypernatural intent he could not decipher.

In a hotel in San Ignacio, Mexico, Zeke and Cindy picked up where they left off in Denver, making a bed move across the floor and back again. Cindy rented the entire top floor of the Howard Johnson's, the only hotel in town, for privacy after Zeke phoned her from Phoenix. Jonny Quarrels had mentioned this little hideaway during one of their weekly dinners while making small talk about a suit he had filed on behalf of investors. Besides Strauss, however, who was ensconced with a case of tequila and his maps and notebooks and a TV satellite feed in a room at the far end of the hall, they were the only ones in the hotel, except for the help and they were hardly ever seen.

The Disney and McDonalds Corporation had contracted with Howard Johnson to build this cube of rooms on the sea, in this sleepy village forty miles from the base of the Sierra Madre Occidental, so that all parties involved in a proposed destination resort and theme park, Borderland, could stay on site in comfort.

Although the resort was nearly 200 miles south of the U.S., it was supposed to be a re-creation of the Mexican illegal migrant experience, an irony that seemed to elude its planners. There were to be rides like a water slide named "The Rio Grande" complete with an artificial river of knee-to-chest-deep water at the bottom, although it was to be clear and chlorinated instead of brown with rainbows of oil on its surface like the real river, and an obstacle course of chain link fences with a replica of the California freeway at the end where the tourists would have to dodge big cushioned plastic cars happily operated by other theme park visitors. There were also darkened desert landscapes planned that would be housed in great air conditioned Quonset huts, blocks long, where

150

spotlights sliced through the air and Borderland employees screamed through bullhorns and mechanical coyotes howled. These particular "recreation experiences" were envisioned by the planners as a kind of participatory board game where theme park visitors gained points, depending on how far they got in the obstacle course, that they could apply toward the purchase of overpriced souvenirs in the multitude of gift shops in Borderland's "town square," a capitalist nirvana in miniature to represent what the poor and huddled masses around the globe deemed America itself.

McDis Corp., the newly formed holding company for the project, had run into unexpected problems, however. Although they successfully navigated the labyrinthine Mexican bureaucracy and acquired all the state-owned land they needed, although they had bribed San Ignacio's mayor to get building permits and to represent McDis Corp.'s plans to the peasant populace, the people of San Ignacio had been less than impressed. Not that their disapproval in-and-of itself meant anything to the corporation, but they needed employees and the townspeople's reaction had bordered on general insurrection.

San Ignacio was a mining boom town, built on the sight of a 17th century Spanish mission which was built on an ancient Tarahumara burial ground. The mine went bust fifty years ago when the silver ore ran out. Those who stayed after the mine stopped producing had reverted to herding, goats mostly and a few cows, and the land where the new theme park was to be located served the community as a kind of commons where their small herds wandered and fed and drank from the several springs. The locals also gathered roots there to supplement their diet and herbs to heal the sick.

The mayor explained to the people from the church steps that the McDis Corp. had their best interests at heart. Not only was Borderland a way for middle class gringos to better understand the plight of poor Mexicans, with its constructed "village" of thatched

151

adobe filled with ragged children and one-eyed women begging for change in front of the shops that would sell McDis Corp. merchandise, and here the mayor paused dramatically and held up a multi-colored serape and put on a straw sombrero with the theme park logo on it, a grinning cow in Mickey Mouse ears, not to mention the consciousness raising message of the rides themselves, but the locals could get jobs working the concessions and wouldn't need cows and goats and herbs ever again. They would all be swimming in Norte money.

"...and you will no longer be peasants," he said finally and raised his fist like Zapata.

Someone in the crowd hit him in the eye with a rock and someone else set fire to his likeness made of straw and old clothes and someone else brandished a machete and a coil of rope. The mayor hid under the altar in the church all that day and fled to Mexico City under cover of dark to wait out the people's wrath. That was many months ago, and he still didn't dare to return.

The McDis Corp. built the hotel anyway, at great expense since all labor as well as most of the materials had to be flown in, believing they could eventually buy the peasants'' complicity, that they would all want jobs at the theme park/resort when they saw how much money the staff at the Howard Johnson's made.

Even though they found a handful of local women willing to be maids, however, and a few young men to be bellhops and bus boys and clerks, the concept of service was not as inherent to poor people as the corporate executives believed. The Disney employees the corporation flew in to train the locals were thorough and patient, indulgent even, but after two weeks they flew back to the states and the new maids and bellhops, et al. showed up every two or three days, then once a week, and finally almost not at all.

The executives were still trying to figure out if the locals were incapable of understanding the gringo need for constant subservient attention and cleanliness and order, or if they were

152

baiting the corporation, showing McDis that they would not be a compliant work force.

The board in charge of planning the new resort had formed a committee to explore the possible positive outcome of absolute chaos in San Ignacio, and another to explore possible ways to bring that chaos about, from brucellosis infection of the goat herds to the disappearance of local children, both of which could be tied to primitive superstition and witchcraft, but the bottom line was that the Howard Johnson's was a mess and the top people at McDis Corp. were having second thoughts about their destination resort. To top it all off, the company's own investors were suing them for what amounted to fiscal stupidity. Very embarrassing.

At the end of Zeke and Cindy's first week together in the Howard Johnson's (a week nearly idyllic for both of them, a honeymoon of physical and emotional bliss, except for Strauss' constant badgering that they needed to move on and Zeke's growing but as of yet unexplained uneasiness), after the Borderland brigade had been gone for at least two weeks, the signs of McDis Corp.'s last corporate meeting were still everywhere: empty scotch bottles and half eaten plates of food giving birth to fly larva (mostly chateaubriand and scallops prepared by McDis Corp.'s own chefs-Mexican cuisine aside, the executives refused to eat typical Howard Johnson fare) and used condoms in overflowing garbage cans. There were even a pair of 2 foot long red shoes that a McDonalds clown, who had been brought along to entertain the executives, left behind when he was forced to flee San Ignacio unexpectedly after the locals mistook him for an agent of the devil, one of the supernatural entities from their ancient mythology that had been relegated to the other team when the missionaries chose up sides. They tried to hit him with baseball-bat-sized crosses, to knock him back over the threshold of darkness where all demons belong, and the corporate body guards barely managed to sneak him out of town long enough to get out of his costume and to the makeshift airstrip.

Cindy got a kick out of straddling Zeke backward while he wore nothing but those big red shoes. Zeke had previously believed that Cindy must certainly have shared the entire range of her nocturnal-animal-like noises with him in Denver, but their third day of nearly nonstop lovemaking, the day Cindy discovered the shoes in one of the room's closets while looking for anything that might resemble a clean towel, she laughed and barked like a hyena all the way to orgasm, over and over.

Zeke didn't get it, what the attraction could possibly be, or how laughter and orgasm were related. In fact, at first he was appalled and self conscious. Perhaps there was some symbolic commentary on his manhood or his lovemaking he was not smart enough to figure out. He was too enthralled by the position, however, to care for very long.

****

"The people I'm working with in the Sierras are mostly Apache," said Strauss, "descendants of runaways from the San Carlos reservation in Arizona, but a few are descendants of the Apache indigenous to the Mexican Sierras, a warrior race who drove whites and Mexicans crazy from here to the border during colonization."

Strauss had taken on the cooking chores for all three of them shortly after they arrived. The hotel refrigerators had been scavenged by the help, but there were two large walk-in freezers filled to overflowing with meat and fish hidden behind a false wall in one corner of the basement that Strauss had discovered while exploring. Only someone with archaeological training could have found it, he said.

For tonight's meal he had cooked beef brochettes marinated in an exotic sauce of his own invention made of plantains and yams purchased at the open air market. It was a little sweet for Zeke's tastes, but he chased each bite with cheap Mexican *cerveza*. which muted the effect. Cindy ate hers hungrily. Love making, she was certain, was the mother of appetite.

"There are a few other tribes represented too though," Strauss continued. He had finished his meal and was sipping on one of the cans of beer and patting his stomach with his free hand. The large dining room echoed with the absence of other guests.

"...Some Plains Indians, a Cree guy, an Athabascan, but most of the non-Apache are from the Southwest tribes, Navajo and Hopi."

Strauss belched, his hand over his mouth in a meager attempt to be polite. Zeke stacked Cindy's empty plate on his and carried them to a table near the back of the dining room where all the others they'd dirtied were piled, a cairn of cheap plates and glasses and knives and forks covered with copulating flies.

"They're a strange lot, really," Strauss continued when Zeke returned to his seat. They're more like a millennial movement than an actual tribe, more a kind of cult I guess than Indian romantics or vestigialists.

"They believe the beginning of the end of white rule occurred on the last day of the 20th century, that all whites will eventually disappear and all the wild game reappear, as will the ghosts of all Indians killed by whites, directly or indirectly. The apparitional ancestors will howl together in one long discordant tremolo of triumph and grief and then rest peacefully, finally."

"So how do they explain you?" asked Cindy. "I mean, you're obviously white. How is it they consent to be studied?"

"I'm not there to study them," said Strauss. "As far as the granting agency is concerned I'm using their money to look for the last remnants of Yaqui healing rites somewhere in central Mexico. That's true, but I'm really in the Sierra to help these people recover what is lost."

"What do you mean?" asked Zeke. "If there are Apaches here who have been here all along, they must know something about the kind of things an anthropologist could tell them."

155

"Subsistence-wise, yes...but I'm there to teach them ceremonies mostly, which is damned ironic, obviously. I met one of these people when I was working with the Navajo in Arizona and he asked me to come to the Sierra and teach the people all I could about Native American ceremonies of any kind, regardless of the tribal culture they come from.

"The people who grew up in the mountains know what to eat from the wild and how to cultivate corn and oats at incredible altitudes and how to hunt. In fact, the arrival of people from other tribes has helped them cope even better in regard to subsistence than previous generations. The Southwest peoples brought great pottery making and weaving skills, the Plains people brought bow and arrow making, the Athabascan is one hell of a fisherman..."

"But they have no holy people," interrupted Zeke. He was thinking about Beak and Cantarita's mother, the services, both spiritual and medical, they provided their people. He wondered if they knew about Strauss' "tribe."

"Exactly," said Strauss, "or at least they didn't. That apocalyptic-utopian prophecy is kind of in the air, so to speak, as nearly as I can tell anyway, among tribals all over the Americas. I've heard more or less the same version of the end of white civilization from Canada to the deserts of central Mexico, and rumors it is talked about at least as far as Guatemala, so they didn't need a shaman for that portion of their religious beliefs, but nearly everything else had been lost: songs, ceremonies, dreams, rites-of-passage...."

Strauss belched again and opened another can of beer. He tossed his empty in the general direction of the cairn of plates and glasses and silverware.

"There is a holy man among them now, however. Fuentes. He just showed up one night a little over a year ago as I was trying, in my limited way, to keep a woman in labor alive. The baby was breach, and I was pondering having to reach up there and turn it. Both mother and child were also toxemic. The old woman, Luisa, who is a midwife and herb gatherer, was certain the baby would die, of shock if nothing else, and the mother's prognosis wasn't good either, but Fuentes just walked out of the wilderness, right into the Plains-style tepee where the woman was laying, and started chanting and burning herbs and making tea. Mother and child are still with us and so is Fuentes.

"So, they don't need you anymore?" asked Zeke. The question was self-serving. He obviously didn't understand the need for an anthropological apprentice if the tribe no longer needed an anthropologist.

"That's debatable," said Strauss. "I call Fuentes the Coyote, after the trickster, because I think he's part con-man, though maybe most shaman are, manipulators of consciousness via sleight of hand and other hocus-pocus. Anyway his methods are really syncretic, which is partly why he fits in so well, but also why the people at the encampment still need me, to contextualize his techniques, if nothing else, so the people are not accepting or rejecting them in a vacuum. A cultural trait without a viable context is just a museum piece, a dead artifact.

"He uses a suck tube, for example, to draw out evil like they do further south, but some of his songs are from the Sundance which is a Plains ceremony, and then there's stuff I don't recognize at all. Fuentes, the Coyote, hinted once that his magic was Olmec, older even, but who knows. Fuentes himself is Catholic."

"Catholic?!" Zeke and Cindy said in unison.

Zeke could see his mother in his imagination holding her face in her hands and turning pale at the thought of her beloved Mary, mother of Christ, in cahoots with a magician.

"Yeah. It's not so unusual really. Catholicism and the old ways are much intertwined in all of Meso-America, and maybe more in and around the Sierras than anywhere else. There is much magic in the church down here and much that is Catholic in the ancient rites as they are still practiced. Whether the man calls himself a shaman or a Christian is merely a matter of emphasis for him."

157

****

While he was shopping that afternoon for the ingredients to the meal they had just eaten, Strauss said, he heard a rumor that Fuentes was in town. He suggested Zeke go with him to mass the next morning to meet the old man.

"If the Coyote is in San Ignacio, he will certainly be at mass on Sunday morning. He never misses when he has the chance, predictable as a full moon. He has a lot of pull at the encampment now, and any outsider, especially a white man, will have to meet with his approval before going there."

"He must mistrust you as much as you mistrust him," said Zeke. "Why else would he stop me if I'm with you?"

But Strauss said he had to pee and needed his rest besides and would bang on Zeke's door early, and he left the dining room without answering.

The world tilted like a carnival ride before Strauss's footsteps were beyond hearing in the long hallway leading out of the dining room and into the kitchen. Zeke heard the deep and angry roar of thunder in his inner ear, the typical prelude to a waking vision like Zeke had not experienced in many days, but Cindy cut the rumble off mid-stride and tipped the world bolt upright when she giggled, a little tipsy from the beer, squeezed him hard between the legs, and asked him to wear the big red shoes, just one more time.

It is almost ludicrous, thought Zeke, how the possibility of sex could so alter the fabric of the universe.

****

The church where Zeke and Strauss went in search of Fuentes was made of three foot sided white stone cubes quarried 10 miles to the east, and huge round wooden beams from the Sierras whose first slopes were twenty or more miles beyond that. The materials

158

were hauled here, according to Strauss, by conscripted Tarahumara Indians in 1654 so the Spaniards would have an appropriate sacred space where they could meet their soul-hungry God.

The pew at the back where Zeke and Strauss sat was not as old, Strauss said, by a hundred years, give or take a hundred years, thought Zeke, but still ancient and still hard as granite.

The priest at the altar, cassocked and surpliced, held his arms out like the full-sized sacrificial Christ that hung behind him. The priest spoke the mass in Spanish, elegant and syncopated like English is only in the mouths of some few poets; Christ bled, and it was not some abstraction of blood, but sanguine enough that Zeke had to look very hard from this distance to be sure it was not really blood, some pomo-art version of the crucifixion, as outlandish as the prospect seemed in this place.

But it was Christ's expression that held Zeke's attention. There was pain in that carved face, ineffable human agony. The cathedral in Denver where Judy's funeral was held had several crucifixes hung around the place, but Jesus' expression was either beatific, his eyes raised toward the sky, or his head hung limp, eyes closed as if he were peacefully, blissfully even, dead.

This Mexican Christ, this Christ with burnished skin and black Mexican or Indian hair, bleeding with pigment of the Earth applied and reapplied over generations so that blood of his wounds was truly blood-colored, knew horror, knew the pain of the flesh, knew this single rail he rode like a train was headed toward the ineluctable dark.

Zeke wondered, is this the pain of leave-taking? Is this poisoned garden still so much something to behold among all the worlds that, no matter how empty or exalted the reason for leaving, leaving is always heart rending, always the remorseful last act of a generally remorseless species?

A wave of déjà vu swept over Zeke so quickly he lost his equilibrium completely and slumped forward. Strauss caught him and pushed him gently back against the pew, a look of concern on his face that bobbed in Zeke's peripheral vision.

"Death," whispered Zeke. "There will be a death here, soon." Strauss looked confused now, as well as concerned.

The ancient carved doors of the cathedral stood open just behind and to the right of where Zeke and Strauss sat to let in what little breeze blew off the high desert. The priest's voice faltered and the congregation, all on their knees except for Zeke and Strauss, turned toward the back of the church as a single being. Two men with automatic weapons stood on either side of the door. They were dressed incongruously in tailored suits and shiny black cowboy boots in a church filled with people in denim and calico and cheap hemp sandals.

Another man walked in the door, equally impeccably dressed, his fine shoes so polished and buffed they reflected the light from the brass basin of holy water he stood next to. He held a large semi-automatic pistol in his right hand.

The man with the pistol removed his sunglasses and handed them to one of the other men. Zeke had seen such eyes only once, on his last visit to Uncle Earl in Attica. On his way to the visiting area he had passed a man in manacles. An armed guard sat on either side of him. His eyes were like a veiled fire, somehow piercing but also unseeing, as if he looked through whatever was before him to some presence outside the tangible world, as if his focus were so total that he was all singular, consuming, murderous purpose. Zeke had thought he was merely crazy, a mad killer maybe, but when he mentioned this in passing to his uncle, the older man insulted him, something he had never done before.

"Don't be stupid," he said. "Any man can look that way if he sees too much, if he sees too far, if he looks too hard into things."

The man at the back of the church dipped the fingers of his right hand in the holy water and made the sign of the cross. An old Indian man who had been kneeling in the front row rose solemnly, made the sign of the cross himself, and bowed to the priest who still stood at the altar with his arms spread. Christ's look of horror had now descended on the priest's face too.

Strauss started to stand, but Zeke instinctively held his arm. He knew what would happen here, and he knew what would happen if Strauss tried to interfere.

The old man walked to the first station of the cross and bowed slowly, made the sign of the cross, then walked to the next and bowed. The man with the pistol walked behind Zeke and Strauss to the side aisle and toward the old man who walked to the next station, Jesus Falls for the Third Time. Zeke remembered it from his dream, but also from the Cathedral of St. John in Denver where Judy was eulogized. It was the station he could see most clearly, the one he and Marianne had sat closest to.

The old man crossed himself and turned to meet the man with the pistol. He smiled at him, not benevolently exactly, but like he had a secret. Then he gazed over the heads of the still kneeling, and frightened, congregation and looked directly at Zeke and Strauss. He smiled even more broadly, his worn brown teeth showing.

The gunman grabbed his arm and pulled the old man to him violently and whispered something. Zeke could hear only a rasp like insect wings buzzing in the absolute silence of the parishioners. The old man cackled like it was a joke he'd just heard, like he was crazy, then smashed the gunman square in the face with his fist.

The two men by the door moved toward the side aisle, but the one on the floor yelled "stop" in English, in a near New England accent thought Zeke, and got up slowly. The fire in his eyes was a sustained flash point now as he wiped the blood from his nose over his cheeks, smearing his face into a mask.

"Are you human?" Zeke heard himself whisper. "Damn," he heard Strauss say, "it's all but done now."

The man with the pistol pulled the old man by the front of his shirt until the two were face to face, nose touching nose, put the

161

pistol under his stubbled chin and pulled the trigger. The station of the cross, the fallen Christ, was smeared with pieces of the old man.

The gunman walked out, the shooter's strange eyes seeing nothing, or maybe seeing things no one else in the room knew were there.

****

"I asked Fuentes once where he came from," said Strauss on the church steps as the priest gave the old man last rites inside.

"He said the sky and laughed. So I said, OK smart ass, but what about just before you came to this encampment in the Sierras. From under the Earth, he said then, and he was so goddamn serious it was unnerving after his flippant response seconds before, and I let it drop. I guess he's about to go home."

Zeke had wanted to ask Strauss about what they had just witnessed, but he seemed on the verge of tears, as if he were genuinely fond of the guy he'd christened the Coyote out of suspicion for his motives, and Zeke left him to make arrangements for the old man's remains.

"How did you know?" Strauss asked, as Zeke walked down the stairs.

"I have to check on Cindy," Zeke said, "She'll be awake by now and maybe heard the shot. She'll be worried." He kept walking. How to explain his so-called gift, the knowledge that always seemed to arrive too late, to a man whose friend the knowledge could have saved if Zeke only knew what to do with these strange messages before it was all but over? But then again maybe Judy had been right. What he witnessed in his mind only minutes before the old man lived out the vision of his untimely end was just one possibility among many. Maybe the only real news was of Coyote's impending death, if not here and now then somewhere else and soon. The thought was not comforting. He felt

162

nearly as helpless as he did when Judy fulfilled his prophecy to the letter.

When Zeke left Cindy that morning she was buried under the covers, her favorite position for sleeping. She had told him in Denver that she felt secure this way. They had discussed the future late in the night, a concept still strange, even unreal to Zeke. Cindy said she must check on her phone sex business soon, but planned to buy a house in San Ignacio where she and Zeke could meet as long as he was Strauss' research assistant. Zeke still felt compelled to go on, to move into the mountains with Strauss, although he could not explain it to himself, let alone to Cindy. She thought he just needed something to do, purpose she called it, when he stumbled through his recitation about fulfilling his obligation to Strauss, and he had trembled at the recognition, inchoate but strong, that she was more accurate than she knew when she used that word. He did not know what waited in the Sierra, and so did not know whether they could ever have a future, but the thought of a place to share was a good thought and he let Cindy plan. How they would contact each other, or if they would have a regular schedule, like every other weekend, Cindy said they could figure out later.

Cindy was sitting on the edge of the bed in her bra and panties when Zeke returned. She was crying, and a small stream of blood ran from the corner of her mouth. There were finger shaped bruises on her right arm. She ran to Zeke and embraced him.

"I heard a shot," she said. "I thought those assholes didn't believe me."

"Who?" Zeke asked, but immediately he swooned with memory and had to lean against the corner of the dresser. The effects were cumulative, two flashbacks in so short a time, or maybe the further south he went the stronger these experiences became, the more frequent too, and the weaker he became, hopeless of staving them off even momentarily. His gift, as others

163

had referred to it, was starting to feel like a full blown, full time disability.

"You're hurt," Cindy said as she helped him to the bed. Zeke's ears rang like church bells and he barely heard her words.

"One was a tall man in wrap-around sunglasses and an overcoat," Zeke said. "The other was smallish with bad teeth and a nerve-grating laugh, a cartoon character's laugh. He goes by Weasel." The church bells were now in sync and banging like Charlie Watts on the high hat.

"You were expecting these guys?" asked Cindy. She was worried about Zeke's health, he was still pale as a dead man, though he looked less dead than even a few seconds before, but if he knew these men were coming and didn't tell her she might hurt him herself.

"No, well, kind of," said Zeke. "Did they hurt you?" He wiped blood from Cindy's mouth with the corner of the sheet. His balance was returning and he could hear a little better now. Charlie Watts had joined a marching band and was half a block away.

"I told them to take a flying fuck at the moon when the little one asked where you were, so the big one back handed me. They left when I told them you headed for the mountains a few hours ago. Who are these jerks, Zeke?"

Zeke looked almost himself again and Cindy's lip was starting to throb. She was nearly certain that Zeke could have warned her about these things, each pulse of pain from her lip to her brain made her more certain. The honeymoon-like bliss of the last several days was beginning to fade.

"Bounty hunters from Denver. I remember them now."

"Remember!?" Cindy yelled. "The big one had a sawed off shotgun in his coat. How the hell could you forget somebody like that?"

"We both have to get out of here as soon as possible," said Zeke. "Weasel and his companion will be back in little over half a day. They will ask an old man and woman who live out of doors

164

under a giant cottonwood tree at the base of the Sierras if any gringos have passed that way. They'll know you lied, because they will rough up the old man to make sure he is telling the truth. The old woman will cry and swear to Santa Maria, and Weasel and the big one will turn back...."

Cindy was still angry, but she had to pause, to look at Zeke as if seeing him for the first time. This was, at the very least, an aspect of him she hadn't experienced. True, they had spent much more of their time together growling and groaning and producing the rhythmic unspoken language of flesh slapping flesh than talking, so maybe he was prone to making hypothetical projections as if they were absolute truth; but she couldn't help hearing Kalish's mysterious tone in his certainty, an intimation that he knew things seemingly impossible to know, and knew them beyond a shadow of a doubt.

Zeke stumbled to the bathroom for a packet of Howard Johnson's complimentary Tylenol. Cindy followed him and checked her torn lip in the mirror as Zeke ripped the package open and emptied the pills into his mouth.

"How do you know about the old couple?" she asked as he chased them with water. "I mean, have you been here before?"

"I saw it all," said Zeke, "in a dream at Cantarita's mother's place on the reservation."

Except for Judy, who had discovered his strange abilities by accident and for whom the attribute was a philosophical fascination, and except for Beak who recognized it in him somehow without being told, and for whom the recognition was ultimately disappointing, no one else knew about Zeke's "gift." Cindy deserved to know. She was hopelessly entangled in the bizarre web of his life. She might think he was crazy and leave now, for good, but that would be his gift to her. Her life would be less complicated. She would be safer. Besides, his compulsion to move further south was becoming stronger, and how far he must go before he felt like he could finally stop was an open question.

For all he knew he might end up in Tierra del Fuego, squatting by a fire as icebergs from Antarctica floated past.

"Who the hell is Cantarita?" asked Cindy. Their present dilemma, the shot she heard and Zeke had yet to explain, the renewed trickle of blood seeping around the corner of her mouth, Zeke's weird, prescient-sounding assertions were all secondary now. Cindy doubled her fists.

"I saw you in the same dream," said Zeke. "I thought it was memory, the love making, your beautiful little body next to mine in Denver, but now I know it was a vision...."

He was obviously stalling her, she thought. He obviously didn't want to tell her about this Cantarita, or was it the mother he didn't want to talk about? He had admitted lusting for his wife's mother to Cindy in Denver, during one of their rare conversations. Maybe he had a thing for older women, especially for the mothers of the women he made love to. The complexity of possible reasons to attack Zeke began to overwhelm her. Then the prospect of Zeke with her own mother occurred to her, and she was more appalled than mad. The mental image of Zeke on top of her overweight, and seemingly sexless mother, her paisley house dress to her waist, made Cindy queasy.

"We haven't much time," Zeke said. "It must suffice to say that I am prone to dreams and visions of the future, and they're never wrong. I know you must get to the airstrip and take the plane you hired back to Mexico City, that there is danger between here and there, but you must go now.

"Go with me, Zeke."

"I can't. Your danger would increase. I have no way of knowing if these bounty hunters have officially announced their presence to the authorities, and, if so, whether or not the police down here are looking for me too. I have to get Strauss to leave for the Sierras now as well, without telling him why. I doubt our anthropologist friend would care to hear about my dreams and visions, and I don't know what will happen if he knows the reason

166

the bounty hunters are after me. But getting into the Sierra Madre is the only way. I can't imagine these city boys would follow me into the wilderness."

Cindy knew their time together must end soon, but she was tempted to ask for the red shoes one more time, or to ask for a succinct version of Zeke's psychic autobiography. She settled for a single question, and no one was going anywhere until she got an answer.

"Who is Cantarita?"

Chapter 28

The Coyote's body was frozen hard as rock and wrapped in a sheet. Strauss and some of the locals had hauled his remains to the Howard Johnson's, put him in one of the high tech walk-in freezers the help had emptied after the executives headed home, and cranked it up to quick-freeze.

Zeke and Strauss loaded the old man into the camper a few hours later and tied him to a table leg that was bolted to the floor so he wouldn't roll around on their trip the encampment.

Zeke had not wanted to explain to Strauss why they needed to leave town. He wasn't sure exactly why he didn't want to, whether because Strauss might turn him out on his own if he knew about the bounty hunters, or if he knew that Zeke was a murderer, or if it was the possibility that Strauss would understand the jealous-husband-shoots-cheating-wife thing in some esoteric anthropological context. The first possibility meant being caught, or maybe killed, and the latter seemed more plausible somehow, though Zeke tried in vain to discount the extent to which there was any déjà vu energy in the intuition, but the second possibility seemed the more frightening now.

Chance, former professor of something-or-other and self proclaimed intellectual, failed to identify any vestigial urge Zeke could rationalize as his motive, which was enough for Zeke to find the explanation unsatisfactory. And he no longer wanted to believe his murder of Marianne and the plumber was in any way natural. He still did not understand his act or his modicum of remorse, but it was easier now to believe himself an anomaly, an evolutionary accident, than to assimilate the terrible implications if the taking of life was endemic to the species. Even if murder was merely an atavistic response of the male ego to the betrayal of his wife-as-property and something an anthropologist might well recognize, that made it still a natural human act, part of the human condition inevitably and irremediably, and the thought that Strauss might understand his murders in this light made him shudder.

He preferred at this point in his journey toward whatever fate awaited him to believe Beak wrong too. Death may be the unconscious condition of Western Civilization, but only a few bleak souls were actually Death's agents, like himself and the men in the church with their fine suits and automatic weapons. Accidents in the cosmic scheme, abnormalities, mutants.

But Zeke didn't have to say anything at all to Strauss about leaving, let alone explain his own circumstances. "The people need to know," was all Strauss said as he urged Zeke to finish saying good-bye to Cindy, who waved as they drove away after promising Zeke she would get out of San Ignacio herself as soon as possible.

****

The road that ran due east from San Ignacio to the Sierras was initially good gravel, and Strauss drove up it at 60 miles per hour. The dual wheeled truck raised a cloud of dust that would not settle for an hour.

"Who were those guys who killed Fuentes?" Zeke asked. He was curious, but he also wanted to think about something other

168

than Cindy, since he was unsure whether he would ever see her again,. For once, he would have gladly suffered the sensual disorientation of a waking vision if it told him they would be together eventually. He still had a headache from all of the déjà vu energy he had withstood in so short a time, and thinking about losing Cindy for good made it worse.

"*Narcotraficantes.*"

"Why would they kill an old Indian?"

"That's a long story," said Strauss, "but since going to the encampment may be the most dangerous thing you've ever done, I guess you deserve to know." Strauss sounded nearly apologetic.

Zeke wanted to laugh at the irony of the assertion, but grew immediately sober at the possibility that what Strauss said could be true. Maybe the plausibility of his own death was not merely self indulgence as Beak had hinted but déjà vu after all, and the bounty hunters had nothing to do with it. Maybe he was really entangled in Strauss' tribe's web and would be murdered like Fuentes. Zeke almost laughed again, but this time a rueful and sardonic laugh. A paradox, he thought, that a man who has killed without remorse can still fear for his own life.

"The one who pulled the trigger is the boss, the cacique, the *jefe*, though I've heard he's just a district *jefe* for the Fontes cartel. His name is Chico Silva, but he goes by Chuck, a name he took when he was at Yale in the 70's. I guess Chico isn't a Yale-like name.

"I looked him up in an old yearbook in the basement of the library when I was up there as a guest lecturer 7 or 8 months ago. He looked pretty innocuous among all his rich, white frat brothers, but Chuck is the meanest bastard on Earth as far as I know."

"But why kill Fuentes?"

"Chuck grows poppies not far from the encampment, and about a year ago he tried to divert the creek the people use for water to irrigate his fields, so he could increase his yield. Fuentes went to talk to him at his compound at the foot of the Sierras, but Chuck told him to fuck himself, which I guess offended the old Coyote's Catholic sensibilities." Strauss laughed.

"So Fuentes cast a spell on Chuck right there in his own living room. Two days later, Chuck's infant son, his only child, died. Some hitherto unheard of fungus killed all the poppies that year as well, and every time Chuck turned around something happened to his pot shipments, which he grows in the Sierras too. Several were interdicted, as the DEA guys say, a couple were hijacked by the competition, and one truck was even hit by lightning and exploded. Chuck is nominally Catholic too, but I doubt it ever occurred to him that this was old fashioned divine retribution. Most Christians who are as superstitious as he is, would interpret lightning bolts as the hand of God.

"Anyway, Chuck took to harassing the people at the encampment, taking pot shots at them at first, but later on kidnapping and torturing them before sending them back with missing fingers and broken bones to warn the others, to warn Fuentes to take the spell off.

"Rumor has it that Chuck also took to using magic to defeat Fuentes. Shortly after his kid died, as the story goes, he imported a shaman from the south, but then one of his trucks full of dope was stolen by banditos who apparently mistook it for a shipment of food, since stealing for them was not a for profit scheme but a form of subsistence. Supposedly Chuck had the thieves killed and executed the shaman himself.

"Then he kidnapped a couple of Tarahumara holy people, but the speculation is that they refused to do what he asked outright. Their bodies were found in pieces a few days later. The latest rumor I heard yesterday in the market in San Ignacio is that Chuck has revived Aztec-style human sacrifice, that he kidnaps people and has their hearts cut out while they're still alive."

"Do you think this is true?" asked Zeke, incredulous at the level of evil the human race was capable of, and he thought briefly

170

of Beak and his accusations. He thought: if he himself was an anomaly, what was Chuck? The practice of killing people to influence the universe, Zeke knew, was ancient, and maybe born of some deep recognition of human participation in reality on a large scale; or maybe it was merely the result of egotism that bordered on madness, that was madness. How could any person, or class, or entire culture believe themselves so important?

Zeke was not Chuck, he tried to assure himself...or was the scale merely different? In some essential way weren't they guilty of the same thing? Maybe Chuck was even, at one level, less culpable than Zeke: he at least believed in some purpose in the deaths he caused, however selfish, however ridiculous the cause and effect relationship seemed.

"If it was anybody else," said Strauss, "I'd say this was tribal-superstition-run-wild, but I've not only come to realize that Chuck doesn't need to understand the context of any religious or magical practice to attempt to use it, but this guy has a greater capacity for harm than anyone I know of. Whatever the truth of Fuentes' shamanic power, Chuck is obviously a believer, and a desperate one at that.

"There is a certain desperation in doing in Fuentes himself. He has at least a hundred armed men at his compound and guarding his crops, but he chose to kill the old man himself in front of witnesses and in a church."

"He'll get away with it, won't he?" asked Zeke. He almost laughed out loud one more time at the irony of the question. He didn't know Fuentes, but wanted Chuck to pay for the murder; he obviously knew Marianne, but...

Strauss did laugh, cynically. "Not only will no one who was in the church testify, either out of an understandable desire for self-preservation or in the sincere belief that anyone who could murder in a church must be demonic, there will be no investigation. The *federales* in this district work for Chuck too."

171

The truck hit a pothole that slammed both Zeke and Strauss into the roof of the cab. "Shit," Strauss yelled and down shifted. Both men put on their seat belts.

"Is this the...main way, the road most people take into and out of the mountains?"

"Yeah, the main way. Why?" Zeke could see suspicion in Strauss' face.

He had expected the deteriorating condition of the road to be sufficient reason for the question, but Strauss was obviously on his guard after Zeke's behavior in the church. In truth, Zeke didn't want to run headlong into Weasel and his friend on this narrow road. He wasn't sure what he expected when they left San Ignacio and headed straight for them. Maybe that there were other ways. But he had to let Strauss know the danger.

Zeke remained as vague as he could about why he was wanted, and didn't know how he would answer if Strauss asked, but he told the anthropologist about his pursuers, their visit to the Howard Johnson's, that they were armed. Strauss looked at him now again out of the corners of his eyes but asked nothing. He turned the camper around, which turned out to be harder than Zeke would have expected. The rocks and loose dirt next to the road and the size of the camper meant Zeke had to get out and shout directions while Strauss maneuvered the truck forward and backward until it faced the way they'd come. They crawled back into their own dust for only about a mile, then Strauss bounced the camper hard onto a deeply eroded two-track that headed to the north and east.

"This is a little longer way," he said, "and rougher, but no one will follow you here until they find a guide in San Ignacio. We can get to the encampment by nightfall, and the people will protect you in the short term...but they obviously have enough trouble of their own, and I doubt that trouble died with Fuentes. They'll expect you to move on soon."

****

Zeke fell into a subtle depression at what was apparently the utter disappearance of the slim chance of a future he thought he had only hours before. These last brief days with Cindy he almost believed he had escaped his deeds, against all odds, that he had a future in that hopeful, albeit circumscribed, American sense of the word, a job and a lover for the time being. Even if all he could ever hope for was being Strauss' grunt somewhere in the Mexican wilderness and seeing Cindy a few days a month, that was something, maybe far more than he deserved.

He wondered now if, before his time in San Ignacio, or even before he killed Marianne and the plumber, he'd ever thought in future tense. He had merely walked through his days hating Marianne for what she was, a narrow minded commentator on all he was not, wanting Judy against all reason for everything she was that her daughter could not be, reading and selling books, one of the zombies...and explaining away what prophecy was in him as merely part of his perpetual melancholy, a breach of psychological and physiological normality.

"You ever thought about writing a book?" Strauss asked, interrupting Zeke's somber rumination.

They had not spoken for several, slow miles and Zeke was startled by the timing of the question if nothing else, but he also wondered if this was a ploy to discover why bounty hunters were after him, what heinous offense could make them zealous enough to follow him over an international boundary and through the desert and into what Strauss claimed was the most rugged terrain in the hemisphere.

"Chance asked me that question once," said Strauss. "We were nursing hangovers in May's foyer. I told him I lacked the talent, and regretted it even before the words were out of my mouth. I expected him to insult me like usual, to say something like I don't

173

have the talent to do much of anything beyond wipe my own ass with dried cornstalks like an Indian, but he didn't insult me.

"Nonsense, he boomed. He said that a great thinker, though I suppose this was probably egotistically self-referential, that a great thinker once defined writing-as-great-art as the telling of ordinary tales involving ordinary people in their ordinary situations.

"Chance said he intended to write a vast novel himself one day, about May's...and he spread his arms when he said it as if to embrace that little room: the brocade and velvet hung like clichés everywhere, the women and girls lounging in various stages of undress on the gaudy furniture and fanning themselves, waiting for the Sunday morning regulars who would show up after the wife and kids were at church.

"He said he would be the protagonist: Bob-goddamn-Chance as Everyman in the everyday world, an allegory of world history since the rise of late civilization, all desire and commerce."

Strauss removed his dirty straw hat and hung it on the shifter knob. He wiped the sweat from his bald head with a blue bandanna.

"So what about you, Zeke?" he said as he stuffed the handkerchief back into his shirt pocket and replaced his hat. "Certainly a man with bounty hunters on his trail could tell a tale of commerce and desire."

"Maybe," said Zeke, now certain of Strauss' motive, but unsure of how he would answer if the conversation led to a direct question about his crimes. He really did not want Strauss to know more than he already knew. The possibility that he would put Zeke out on the road or explain the murders made him equally nervous.

"Most books sold in America now are entertainments, vignettes for voyeurs, something to hold the reader's attention briefly, to allow them to peek through the curtains into another life and to thereby momentarily escape their own...but few books are published that are at all dangerous, or what you might call real in

174

the sense of dealing with what it is to be a human being in its more or less gory detail."

"So your story is too dangerous?" asked Strauss, his tone a kind of mocking disbelief. Zeke wondered if Strauss merely believed him incapable of such a life, or if this was another ploy, an attempt to bait him into divulging his decadent past.

"Too real, anyway," said Zeke. "Nobody in America can afford to look too closely at life." He hoped by being vague and waxing Chance-like, Strauss would get pissed and give up.

"So you're saying they're afraid to see themselves in you or that some overwhelming truth is in your story or..."

"I don't know what I'm saying," Zeke interrupted. "I ain't no Einstein."

Strauss had a puzzled expression on his face and his mouth was open as if he intended to continue the questioning, but one front tire hit a hole which jarred Zeke's teeth, and Strauss cursed again and downshifted to low. His expression changed to one of total concentration.

The trail was all rocks and holes now, and Strauss' small frame was jerked and thrown from side to side even though he wore a seatbelt. His knuckles were white as he strained to hold onto the steering wheel. The trail had also begun to climb more steeply, and the saguaro and century plants that had given way to scrub juniper and cedar miles before now gave way to several varieties of tall pines.

They had rocked and bounced and climbed for several hours when the truck rolled up and over the crest of a knoll. For a few long seconds Zeke could see only treetops and blue sky and high thin wisps of cloud. He imagined thousands of feet of empty air on the other side, a fall to death amid tangled metal in some boulder field.

His stomach fluttered like a cage full of pigeons as the nose of the truck came down and the ground rose back into view. The trail ahead was the same as the trail behind, all rocks and holes, but

Zeke could see for miles to the east. Wave upon wave of green mountains rolled away into the distance, dark canyon after dark canyon between them, steep and rocky and ominously beautiful. Zeke had never been anywhere so bereft of signs of human passage. He thought of Rilke, that correlation of beauty with terror, but his recognition of the poet's revelation was tinged with the vague sheen of intuition, like a less-than-half-remembered dream.

"We're going to a meadow about halfway below that third crest over there," said Strauss, and he pointed to the southeast." It's probably only fifteen miles or so as the crow flies, but we'll be lucky to make it before dark...."

Strauss stopped short. A man had stepped into the trail twenty yards ahead of them. He was obviously an Indian, with high cheekbones and a prominent nose and sloping forehead. He also had braids to his waist, black with streaks of gray and tied with strands of leather. He carried an AK47 in one hand.

"They must have heard about Fuentes already," said Strauss. "They don't generally post guards this far from the encampment." He shut off the truck and got out to talk to the man with the gun, who had made no move to approach them.

Zeke got out to pee on the rear tire. This place smelled of age, of rot and growth. The odors mixed with the pungence of Zeke's urine and made him feel old too, old as rock. The Indian motioned toward Zeke with his chin, not once but several times, as he spoke to Strauss, then disappeared into the heavy brush beside the road.

"He's pretty pissed I brought you with me," said Strauss, as he pulled himself into the cab by the steering wheel, as Zeke slammed the passenger door shut.

"They've heard about Fuentes, and they also know about your pursuers. In short, they're expecting the shit to fly now, from all directions, that Chuck's *pistoleros* will descend on them, and maybe the *madrinas*, a secret branch of the *federales* the *narcotraficantes* control. They definitely do not want your trouble piled on top of their own."

176

Strauss started the truck and put it in low.

"So I gave Wounded Man my word you'd stay just long enough to deliver the Coyote's body, and maybe to eat something and get a night's sleep, and then you'd move on."

Zeke wanted to ask Strauss if he intended to just turn him out into the wilderness to fend for himself, but he was afraid if he pissed the anthropologist off now after the Indian gave him hell he might turn Zeke out sooner rather than later. He began to wish his "gift" was controllable, that he could at least have a glimpse of what would happen to him in the morning. Regardless of where his path led, it seemed somehow comforting to know. He decided on more subtle questions instead, to look for some symptom in the answer, or the silence, that followed.

"How did the tribe find out about Fuentes before we arrived? We left San Ignacio only a few hours after he died."

"There is a Tarahumara encampment about five miles from where I'm taking you. Actually, Tarahumara is what the Mexicans call them. They call themselves Raramuri, runners.

"I know one warrior who can do 150 miles without stopping, and in sixteen hours or so, on a bellyful of corn and a flask of peyote juice.

"They're a pretty skittish people. They've been persecuted since the Spaniards got here. Now the *traficantes* take shots at them, for sport, but they also conscript them to work in their illegal timber trade. The few times I've seen Tarahumara away from the encampment it's from a distance and they're moving.

"Anyway, as part of their survival strategy they post people in disguise in San Ignacio and several points in between to gather news. They share their information with the encampment I'm taking you to in return for a little goat's milk.

"One hundred fifty miles?" said Zeke. He was unable to mute his skepticism completely.

"Yes. I heard stories about them in college that I thought were myth too," said Strauss. "How the Mexican government recruited

177

winners for the 1920 Olympics and the Tarahumara sent adolescent girls when they heard 26 miles was the longest race, or how in the '28 Olympics the Tarahumara marathoners had to be talked into stopping by race officials-too short, too short, they kept saying as they ran past the finish line.

"But shortly after I got here, a little boy fell sick with severe colitis and was literally shitting himself to death. I knew there was medicine at Alteros, a Jesuit mission seventy plus miles to the south and east, in the heart of the Sierra Madre Occidental, but there is no road. The fathers have everything helicoptered in.

"The boy's folks sent a runner named Socorro to me to ask the name of the medicine. He left right then, in the middle of the night, and by dusk the next day he handed me the vial."

"Is this Wounded Man a Tarahumara?" asked Zeke.

"He's Lakota, from the Rosebud reservation, in the Black Hills, but he'll still beat us to the encampment. All of the people know the game trails up here and can go where they need to faster than a truck."

Zeke had nearly worked up the courage to ask Strauss for a definition of "move on." To where? How? Alone?

But the trail opened out on his side of the truck as they skirted a ridge. Zeke could not see the bottom of the gorge that fell away from his window into darkness, a black crevasse, a lightless abyss. His breath went short, and he let Strauss concentrate on driving.

Chapter 29

"A glitch. There's always a damn glitch," thought Cindy as the guard nudged her through the door. She had just begun to accept, to re-accept, that her life was a math operation, subtraction, negation, at least when it came to men, when she came upon a roadblock manned by federales with submachine guns.

Her first thought was that the guys after Zeke were in league with the local cops, but she also worried that someone had reported her for stealing the Howard Johnson's van. She wasn't exactly inconspicuous. The shiny new vehicle in a land of 60's vintage automobiles and burros would have stood out without the larger than life smiling cow's head in mouseketeer ears on the roof.

When she first arrived at the airstrip outside San Ignacio, she had hired a cab into town, a '67 Chrysler Imperial with seat covers resembling the plastic bubble wrap her phone sex service's computers were bundled in when they arrived from the store; but she couldn't find that taxi or any other, or anyone who seemed to believe there was such a thing in San Ignacio, maybe in all of Mexico as far as some locals she asked were concerned.

She was desperate and the van was just sitting there and the keys were in it, so she borrowed it. She had left a note at the vacant front desk.

She had been attempting to explain this to a large mustached old man in khaki who spoke only broken English, when she saw the pilot she had hired in Mexico City, and who she'd paid handsomely for him to sleep in his plane at the airport until she returned, waving at her and smiling sheepishly from the back seat of one of the police cars. As nearly as she could make out from her informant, the pilot had agreed to fly several pounds of marijuana to Mexico City for a local drug dealer when he returned Cindy there and was being detained for questioning.

By the time she understood this the pilot was standing next to the police car, smoking a cigarette and talking animatedly to two federales who looked at their feet and kicked the dirt like school boys being reprimanded. Cindy had panicked when the pilot pointed at her.

She poked the fat *federale* in the chest with her finger and shouted that she had nothing to do with this. She was certain the pilot was attempting to shift blame to her and did not want to end up in some Mexican hell-hole like Zig, or to get caught here by the

179

bounty hunters after Zeke who, if they were not already in league with the local cops, would be in league with them if they arrived now in order to get the chance to question her again.

The *federale* had merely smiled politely, removed his hat and bowed. He said in his thick accent, "*El Comandante* would like to meet you."

Now here she was, in the office of a greasy little man with a Clark Gable mustache and a lascivious gleam in his eyes.

"Miss Sweet Stuff," he said, and kissed her hand.

Her passport read, Cindy Sweet, not that anyone had bothered to look at it or any other identification since she entered Mexico, let alone at the roadblock. In fact, they hadn't bothered to look in her large purse that she carried over her shoulder, which was her only luggage. Not that there was anything to find-besides identification all she took was her camera, a pair of blue jeans, a few pairs of clean panties and her money. The rest of what she brought from Denver she had donated to a woman in a maid's outfit, the first of the help she'd seen for several days, whom she had met getting off the elevator after saying good-bye to Zeke. But cops always went through handbags and the like. She thought it was an international custom. She had no idea how this man could know her by that other name, unless the bounty hunters had figured out who the woman in the security tape was and relayed the information.

El Comandante poured her a scotch slowly, sensually, as if his pouring were part of some elaborate sex rite.

"I am *Comandante* Fernando Fernandez, but you may call me F.F.," he said as he set the glass on the desk in front of her. He apologized for her rude handlers and thanked her for her "illustrious presence."

"It is not often," he said as he raised his glass in her direction, "that we here at the Prison of the Serpents have a chance to meet someone so famous."

180

****

F.F. was both the head *federale* in these parts and the warden
of the prison where Cindy now found herself. He was obviously
immensely proud of his title because he repeated it many times in
the course of their conversation: *Distrito Comandante de
Federales y alcalde del prisión de los Serpientes.*
 F.F. explained that it was because of his role as District
Commander of the *Federales* that he had seen Cindy in San
Ignacio a few days before on his way to some errand at the base of
the Sierras, but it was because of his role as warden that he
recognized her. The National Director of Prisons had requested he
attend a convention in Denver some months before to investigate
the privatization of prisons, and, besides being unutterably
impressed with the American capitalist genius to make money
from incarceration, F.F. had been wowed daily by Cindy's phone
sex service, in fact several times a day during his two week stay in
Estados Unidos, after seeing a picture of her dressed in a
provocative nighty in an ad in a Denver paper. She had used her
own photo on the advice of her employees who insisted she was as
alluring as any model and any man who saw the ad should believe
the voice on the other end of the phone belonged to none other
than Cindy Sweet Stuff herself. She had used a tripod and timed
shutter release and taken the picture herself, even managing to
replicate the soft light in soft core girlie magazines.
 "I am still paying the Visa bill," F.F. said proudly as he held
the office door for her to begin their tour of the facilities, at least
he called it a "tour." In truth they never left the upper floor, which
was a suite of empty offices along an L-shaped corridor. They
merely went into the rooms, where F.F. pointed out the tasteful
drapes and carpet, and looked out of barred windows down onto
razor wire and exercise yards and across to guard towers filled
with dour men with weapons. The exercise yards were mostly
empty, though here and there despondent men sat in the dirt, alone

181

or in small groups, near the tall block walls or chain link fence that surrounded them or that divided the place into smaller, more manageable spaces.

"Not quite state of the art, like in America," F.F. said, "but someday." He smiled wistfully and Cindy swore he had a tear in his eye.

She was about to ask when she could leave and how she was supposed to get to Mexico City without a pilot, when she looked out one more barred window and into one more yard, at one more group of despondent men, when she saw Zig. He was thinner and looked far older, even at this distance, but he still had his trademark mane of hair. He was talking to a small group of prisoners as only Zig could talk, like a maestro with birds for hands and all notes were 16th notes, like an old time Baptist preacher under the influence of the Holy Spirit and too much caffeine.

Cindy was stunned by this coincidence, by the sheer weight and power of synchronicity. She strained mightily to remain calm and briefly entertained the idea of asking to use the phone and calling Kalish for some hint as to what this could possibly mean. Fate accomplished? And what the hell kind of fate was this anyway? A wave of sheer terror washed over her.

"There are Americans here," Cindy said flatly, her voice surprisingly calm.

"Yes. Mostly for drug offenses. The DEA keeps very close track of them, not because your government is worried about their well-being, but...well, apparently some Mexican wardens can be bribed." F.F. now looked disgusted.

"I, however, have never let a single American out of my prison," and his look of disgust became pride again, "not a living one anyway."

Another wave of terror smashed into her, but Cindy managed to ask for a tour of the rest of the prison, the lower levels, spontaneously. She had no idea why she asked. It wasn't for love.

182

She had realized since Zig's arrest that she hooked up with him for other reasons, loneliness mostly. And she did not ask out of nostalgia since their relationship was so short and, as opposed to her equally short relationship with Zeke, so unintense it nearly did not exist. Zig was just a small blip on the radar screen of memory, but, although she didn't have any idea how she could possibly find him in so large a place without saying something to F.F., who she was certain would never allow it, she sensed it was of paramount importance to see Zig if she could. She thought of Kalish again but was certain the old woman would only aggravate her with more riddles.

F.F. refused Cindy's request even after she explained as a ruse that the thought of all those men behind bars excited her. He merely looked at her skeptically. Like most men, Cindy realized, only F.F.'s own strange appetites made sense to him, and all others were a mystery. No act of imagination, no extrapolation could span that distance.

So Cindy offered to talk dirty to him, for free of course, if he would grant her a tour. F.F. agreed to this without hesitation, enthusiastically.

After five minutes of Cindy's best stuff his eyes bulged and crossed, and he held the edge of his desk as if he might pass out. He held up one hand, palm out, and whispered hoarsely, "Stop...please." As if her silence now were an act of mercy.

F.F. lay face down on his desk for twenty minutes to recover, then led Cindy blissfully to the elevator and down into the bowels of the building. Cindy blinked for several seconds after the elevator doors opened before she could see the guard standing just outside. F.F. spoke to the guard in Spanish, then instructed Cindy to follow the man with the gun down the aisle of iron barred cells. He said he would wait for her upstairs, that the smell disturbed him. The doors closed, and Cindy heard the elevator ascend.

The guard pushed a button and the electric doors that separated the elevator from the cell block opened. The stench that

183

poured over her almost made Cindy retch: sweat and shit and all other human effluvia mixed with ammonia that was obviously too weak to compete with, let alone cover, such a stink.

There were no lights in the aisle itself, but a single small watt, bare bulb hung in every cell. The effect was starkness itself. The concrete and the iron and the straw-filled mattresses and the shit pails were all the color of nightmare, somehow variable tones but with the same cast: despair and horror.

There were three men in every eight-foot-by-eight-foot cell. All were quiet. Except for coughing from somewhere up the row of cells, there was no noise as if this were a church or a ward for the deaf and dumb. The only constant sound was the guard's hollow footsteps on the concrete ahead of her. Cindy reached quietly into her purse for her camera, again without understanding her own motivation in the least, the need to record this place when it put her in danger to make her heart nearly beat out of her chest. She let the guard walk a dozen or so steps ahead, then took pictures of one cell, then the next, and the next. The prisoners turned to her with dull eyes, uncomprehending, beyond affect perhaps.

Then she was before Zig's cell. The odds of finding him at all were outrageous, and she felt her breath being sucked out of her again at the sheer improbability, but here he was: first a look of confusion and shock on his face, then his big stupid grin and his mouth opening, inevitably, to say something. Cindy held her finger to her lips to keep him quiet just before the guard turned to look at her. Whether he heard the camera's winder over his footsteps or was merely checking on her location she wasn't sure.

Cindy put both hands behind her back as if walking studiously so he couldn't see the camera, then motioned with her head that he should continue. As the guard's footsteps began to echo again, she handed the camera to Zig through the bars. She pantomimed that he was to take as many pictures as he could, then hand the camera back to her as she returned up the aisle. Zig nodded his understanding and blew her a kiss.

184

After they had walked another few hundred feet past what seemed like endless pairs of equally desperate eyes, the guard stopped to peer into a cell. When Cindy reached him, she saw a man face down in his own blood and vomit as his cellmates stared at the floor in front of them. He was obviously dead, the one eye Cindy could see rolled back in his head and milky white. The man looked roughly her own age, too soon one of the inconsolable dead, and so filthy he was already halfway to dust before he stopped breathing.

Cindy covered her mouth with her hand to indicate her sickness to the guard and motioned that she wished to leave. She fell several steps behind him again, took the camera from Zig, who blew her another silent kiss, and returned it to her purse without the guard noticing. Zig mouthed, "thank you," as the invisible kiss hovered between them on the air.

Cindy was pale when she exited the elevator at the top floor, at F.F.'s suite of empty offices, but the *Comandante* did not notice or did not care. He told her the pilot was waiting at the airstrip outside San Ignacio as he escorted her to the same car she had arrived in. He kissed her hand once more and thanked her for her services, for her illustrious presence.

He said, as he smiled beatifically, "I would ask you to talk to me again before you leave, but I'm afraid one more time would kill me." He pressed his fingertips to his lips, unwittingly mimicking Zig's kiss moments before.

Cindy could not wait to hear what Kalish had to say about cosmic coincidence. The wrinkled one will probably laugh so hard she'll croak, thought Cindy, and in spite of her nausea, part the result of adrenaline and part fear and part a reaction to what she had seen and smelled, she smiled.

Chapter 30

Helicopters descended from the night sky by the light of the full moon spitting flames like falling angels. Chuck himself hung from the door of the lead machine, death disguised as light leaping from his hands, his mouth forming curses that not even he could hear over the storm of engines and gunfire and blades turning.

Wounded Man and a few others stood in the hail and fired back as the rest dove for cover behind boulders or hid behind log round houses or ran for the forest in the direction from which the choppers had appeared. One helicopter, the second to pass, smoked, turned sideways dumping one man to the ground, and crashed on top of the man and one of the Plains-style tepees in the center of the encampment. The remaining two turned back the way they'd come, firing at the last stragglers to reach the trees, made another pass at the encampment and flew away.

Those who had returned fire reloaded and stared into the darkness. They stood still for many long minutes, straining to hear any indication that the helicopters were returning, before they dared move to help the others tend to the fallen. They buried one man that night, the only Athabascan in the encampment, and Strauss and Luisa Taya, an old Navajo *partera*, a midwife and herb gatherer, tended two other adults and a child.

Wounded Man gave orders to two men in a language Zeke didn't recognize, then in Spanish to two more. The first pair hurried off in the direction the copters had attacked from, and the other two trotted toward the southwest.

"I've sent our two best warriors to the point you said Dominguez and the bounty hunters will show themselves first, and the other two are headed for the Tarahumara camp to ask for their help," Wounded Man said to Zeke before he trotted off to assist Strauss and the *partera*.

Zeke had watched the attack from the doorway of a round house used for storage. He knew it was coming. He had warned the people of Chuck's plans that morning, after having dreamt this very scene the night before. They listened politely, for the most part, because he had also dreamt a cure for Wounded Man's niece, which he had delivered to Luisa Taya via Strauss where she tended the girl in the very tepee where the crushed helicopter now burst into flames.

He dreamt the little girl had long stringy filaments inside her, just below her navel, that he pulled them from her by kissing her there, and that he buried them under the full moon, that the girl would die if this was not done.

"Right. Now you're a fucking gringo shaman," Strauss said, obviously annoyed at being awakened from his sound sleep.

The old woman had looked hard at Zeke as Strauss told her the dream in Spanish. She bowed to him and took some dried herb from a pouch she wore around her neck. She chanted and sprinkled some into the girl's navel and pulled something long and luminous with her teeth from the child's body. She placed the thread in the pouch with the rest of the herb and instructed Strauss to help Zeke bury it in a particular place, on a stream bank several hundred yards from camp.

Then Zeke had slept again, but he awoke before dawn with the certain knowledge that Chuck would attack from the air, and that a smallish man with a knife scar the length of his forearm would lead the bounty hunters here and kill two of the guards on the periphery of the encampment before retreating.

Wounded Man had speculated that morning that the man with the scar was Manuel Dominguez, whose arm was scarred by a whore in Mexico City several years earlier, a whore who died for her indiscretion. Dominguez apparently had a bloody reputation beyond this singular incident, but Wounded Man did not elaborate.

187

He said he had no explanation for Zeke's dream that saved his niece, beginner's luck maybe, but the rest could just as well be a trick. Zeke could have met Dominguez during some shadowy deal making in San Ignacio, or just seen him drinking at one of the taverns, and everyone for 200 miles knew Chuck was a blood thirsty bastard. Wounded Man argued that Zeke just wanted the people's protection as long as he could get it.

"Besides," he had said, and stepped face to face with Zeke, so close he could smell the goats milk on the Indian's breath," who could believe that a "Norte Americano, white fucker with bounty hunters after him has the 'sight,' or would help the people if he did have the power."

For Zeke the fact that he had recognized the contents of a premonition before it was merely déjà vu just prior to an event's culmination was a mixed blessing. He was happy to have saved the girl's life and who knows how many of Strauss' tribe, and he even allowed himself to believe that this was some small recompense for Marianne and the plumber, but he also recognized that this heralded a new relationship to his so-called gift. He felt a far off uneasiness at what lay ahead yet further to the beckoning south.

There was gunfire in the direction from which Dominguez, the Weasel, and the big nameless one with a shotgun in his coat had appeared in Zeke's dream. Wounded Man and a few others hurried through the moonlight and into the dark toward this new danger at a dead run.

In spite of Zeke's warning, and his part in saving the little girl who now sat on his lap in the roundhouse where the wounded were being tended, he knew the people would hold him accountable for this new violation of their safety. He hadn't dreamt that part, but it only made sense. These people's lives in this terrain were probably touch and go sometimes without Chuck trying to exterminate them, let alone without being entangled in his pathetic web as well.

Within minutes Wounded Man and the others returned carrying one of the guards. He was bleeding from his throat where

188

Dominguez tried to slit it. He had only escaped, Zeke learned later, when the two men Wounded Man sent arrived in mid-knife-stroke. The young man held the wound shut with one hand and made abrupt signals at Zeke with the other.

Wounded Man interpreted: "He says, go away...."

****

Zeke dreamt of Marianne that night, that the bullet hole in her forehead was not really a third eye but lips, and the lips whistled a cantata as if to remind Zeke what he had stolen from the world: that atmospheric sound, that strange music.

He awoke in the dark, utterly remorseful for the first time in his life, tears in his eyes, and listened to the prophetically pathetic howl of a Mexican gray wolf over the small rhythm of Strauss' breathing from where the anthropologist slept on the other side of the camper. Strauss had told him on their trip into the mountains that these animals were nearly extinct, as were the jaguar and the thick-billed parrot, as were the Indians. Strauss had grown silent then, but after a few minutes embarked on a tirade worthy of Bob Chance himself about government involvement with the traficantes and their selfish, profit-driven destruction, about how officials knew the forests were being illegally clear-cut, and how they knew of the willful destruction of the locals through virtual enslavement in the growing and logging operations, about how the government pretended the nearly daily murders were apparitions or intertribal animosities turned violent, an inevitable violence born of millennia of mistrust.

"Maybe our anarchist friend, Robert Chance, is right," Strauss had said finally. "The only actual freedom anyone can hope for is in that split second between regimes, in that chaos when all parties privy to power are too busy with each other, attempting to establish their own positions, to kill little people...or maybe even Chance is naive.

189

"There are always the thugs who are really in control no matter what side announces its momentary supremacy, and those guys probably never miss a beat in their exploitation and destruction in the name of making money off of the good people of the planet Earth-bastards like Chuck and his bosses."

"Our malaise made manifest," thought Zeke as he fell asleep again. This time he dreamt, with extraordinary clarity, of nothing, of oblivion, of death from inside it.

****

The people gathered what they could carry and left the encampment the next day. Tarahumara curers took the wounded to a cave a few miles from their camp to tend them until they could rejoin the group. Other Tarahumaras drove the people's livestock to meadows further north along with their own, where Chuck's goons wouldn't think to look, and the remainder of the tribe who called themselves runners went east with the people to establish a common encampment further in the Sierras, hopefully beyond the reach of helicopters.

Strauss left for San Ignacio with the wounded guard in his truck. The man needed medical attention neither the Tarahumara curers or Luisa Taya had time for, since he would need to be bound at the throat and watched around the clock for several weeks, until his throat grew together. Strauss suggested the man be stitched together by the McDis Corp. doctor, a general practitioner the company had flown in from L.A. and who was still in San Ignacio, having fallen in obsessive love with a local widow who ignored him.

Zeke was to head southward, which was some kind of cosmic forgone conclusion as nearly as Zeke could tell, straight down the multiplicitous spine of the Sierra Madre Occidental with Wounded Man, in an attempt to lead the added danger of Dominguez and the bounty hunters away from the rest. Zeke gave Strauss a brief note to forward to Cindy from San Ignacio: I will contact you if I can, but I can't say where I am going because, as usual, I really don't know...except that the trail will be through wilderness.

One more leave-taking, thought Zeke, one more that would seem to be their last. He had thought to send a final good-bye now, then to say he'd find a way to communicate with her come hell-or-high water, then to remind her of the odds against the time they had together in San Ignacio and to hold out hope, then to say nothing at all and just disappear, to do her that favor. In the end he settled for the sublimely innocuous, but what more could a man so pushed by the big hands of circumstance say about the future?

Zeke and Strauss ate a last meal together of Navajo bread and heated goats milk near the smoldering remains of the helicopter. They toasted the painful death of all stupid bastards who would kill the innocent, Zeke wondering if he was destined to live the rest of his days in the pallid arms of irony, and went their separate directions.

****

Zeke and Wounded Man walked nonstop all morning, until Zeke's knees were knots of agony from the continued climb and descent, climb and descent..., and he had to insist on resting, bounty hunters on their trail or not. He carried only a bedroll, having given Cantarita's sleeping bag to Wounded Man's niece, and a small pack with fried bread and some kind of dried fruit he didn't recognize in it. He also carried a small water bag made of an inside out goat's stomach slung over one shoulder by a canvas strap. He had told Wounded Man he was an out of shape city boy who couldn't carry any more than these few things when the Indian insisted he carry a rifle or, at least, a pistol, and now his need for rest probably confirmed the assertion.

It had really only been an excuse, however. The very thought of carrying a gun gave him flashbacks of Marianne and the plumber. He could not even conjure her face in his imagination in Phoenix, but Marianne's face, complete with whistling wound, had come to him wholly unbidden three times since his dream the night before, and he was only barely able to dispel the vision three times with a supreme act of will. To carry a gun would be a continual reminder, and Zeke knew he did not have enough will to hold the vision off continually. He wondered how many more times he could fend it off and when he couldn't, how long he would be able to stand living with Marianne's floating, whistling countenance before he went mad. He had struggled to be a daily mourner, to feel remorse, to hunger for some transparent understanding of what he was guilty of, a small portion of which he had achieved for the first time, however momentarily, the previous night in Strauss' camper; but today he felt merely haunted, like Marianne was exacting her vengeance.

The vision of her contrapuntal wound came over Zeke now, as he and his companion ate bread and fruit in the shade. He pushed the apparition away and fought off the nausea that came with it only after a paramount effort. He focused on the rolling ridges that disappeared into the gray wash of the distance until he felt corporeal again, something close to whole but nearly exhausted. He stretched his legs out on the ground in front of him when the ache returned along with his body. His knees popped.

"Thanks for taking me south," Zeke said. He didn't know where he was going, but he knew he stood no chance in the wilderness without Wounded Man, and that this was a sacrifice for the Indian. Zeke had seen this warrior wipe his tears after saying good-bye to his niece and his sister. This was the first opportunity he'd had to voice his appreciation. Other than Zeke's insistence they stop a few minutes before, neither man had said a word since the encampment.

"It's for the good of the people," said Wounded Man. "Besides, I couldn't leave you to Dominguez, so..."

"I thought you believe I deserve jail, or do you mean you think Dominguez and the bounty hunters would kill me rather than take me back alive?"

"I mean Dominguez would probably chop you up and sell you for spare parts," Wounded Man laughed.

Zeke nearly choked on his mouthful of fruit. He hoped this was a warped euphemism, but somehow he knew it wasn't.

"Dominguez is not merely your enemy. He is the enemy, evil. Hearts, livers, eyeballs...he sells them like carburetors and tires and front quarter panels."

"What the hell are you talking about?" asked Zeke. He wondered if this was something endemic to Indians, extreme statements about evil and the like.

"Strauss didn't tell you?" Wounded Man said through a bite of bread.

"Tell me what?" A wave of panic arrived right behind the wave of déjà vu, and the second wave arrived because the first was so huge. All his other visions in his life, all other dreams were but a minor prelude to this flood of input into Zeke's awareness, into consciousness; but all this knowledge was a morass, an overwhelming whole that refused to congeal to some singular event or truth. Zeke felt as if the entire human universe was washing over him and that he might drown, disappear forever in the flood, sink into the chaos and never surface.

"Your bounty hunters got themselves the best tracker I have ever seen when they hired Dominguez, but they also got something else I doubt they can imagine. The rumor is that Manuel Dominquez is almost single-handedly responsible for the extinction of the Tubares."

Strauss had told Zeke about these people. He claimed to have glimpsed the only remaining two Tubares on a trek deep into the Sierras with Luisa to collect herbs. The old woman had claimed, at any rate, that these were the last two, a man and woman of middle age. She also claimed they were cannibals.

193

Strauss said Luisa made the sign of the cross and sprinkled the dried and crumbled leaves of a plant she said was one of her allies, a plant she refused to name, in a circle around herself and the anthropologist. She said the magic of the plant would protect them.

The man and woman merely circumvented them, according to Strauss, and without so much as looking in their direction, even though Luisa sang a Navajo hymn at the top of her lungs. They just disappeared into the forest. Strauss explained to Zeke that if the Tubares were or ever had been cannibals, they were probably the ritual variety. Some cultures believe a person's body contains their essence, so they cremate the dead and make a drink mixture of the ashes and pass it around to get some of whatever quality the dead one had that made him or her the human being they were. That way the tribe carries the person, and whoever's essence that person had partaken of, and whoever those people partook of, and etc., through their life...and they know their essence will be carried on in the tribe in the same manner after they die. Every member is connected in this way to every other across time and space. Every individual is not just a culture bearer, but an actual bearer of the tribe, a compendium and an incubator all at once, the container of all the tribe's experience and the maker of new experience, new living history.

"Anyway," Strauss had said, "there is no way to tell for sure if the Tubares practiced ritual cannibalism since, according to Luisa, there are only those reclusive two left. Besides, cannibalism, the actual consumption of flesh, is the worst thing a semi-Christianized Indian can imagine, which is damned ironic at a variety of levels since they symbolically eat the body of Christ every chance they get, so maybe they just labeled these recluses, whose standoffish behavior they don't understand, as the worst of abominations."

Wounded Man continued: "The rumor in the Sierras is that Dominguez hunted the Tubares for their hearts and sold them to a deviant Huichol sorcerer in the south who boiled and ate them, but Strauss told me the rumor in Mexico City is that the sorcerer is really an agent for an organ bank that caters to rich *Norteños*, that he carries coolers of dry ice and a powerful two way radio to call in a helicopter so the hearts and other organs get out fresh.

"That's what you think Dominguez wants to do with me?" asked Zeke.

"Both of us probably, if he can catch us, and maybe that's what he wants from the bounty hunters too. I doubt those guys offered him anywhere near the going rate for spare human parts, even one set. If he kills them plus you and me, that's *mucho dinero* times four."

Wounded Man stretched and walked to a spring fifty yards or so from where they had eaten their lunch. He brought back a plain pottery cup of ice cold water a few minutes later and handed it to Zeke.

"You're pretty nonchalant about the possibility of being chopped into pieces and sold," said Zeke. His anxiety had subsided a little, but the chaotic déjà vu energy still surged through him. His sight was charged with it, and he could see every shift of a vulture's feathers where it hung miles away on the wind, could hear the wind in its wings. The essential bird of ill-omen, he thought, though this knowledge should have been beyond him. He wanted to honor that flight somehow, that miraculous bearer of bad tidings, but he did not know exactly how and he had no clue why.

"Actually, the thought is pretty perverse, the idea that part of me might end up inside some gringo, and the transference of energy and knowledge and emotion and power that is in this Lakota body to a white person is even more perverse, but it's kind of interesting too.

"Imagine one of the livers Dominguez stole from a Tubare warrior in the body of some spoiled rock star in L.A. who has managed to dissolve his own. To say that the kind of knowledge in that liver is incompatible with what knowledge is already in the rock star's body is an understatement. The difference between the two is both in quality and in kind; the difference in the depth of their perceptions of the world is immense, unfathomable even.

"The Tubare knows the dreams of jaguars, and those dreams sleep in his liver. He knows the language of plants and birds and how to defeat the demons who live at the bottom of some rivers. The rock star sings about obsessive love, barbiturates, and high priced cars, which I must assume is the breadth and depth of his knowledge. How the hell can he assimilate his new intuition that rocks are alive?"

Wounded Man laughed. "He doesn't," he said in answer to his own question. The rock star goes loco because he has no context for that knowledge except madness. Throw a few animal shaman dreams into somebody who thinks the world is precisely facile songs, gratuitous pussy, and partying until he pukes and he's bound to believe he's a lunatic so much that he actually becomes one."

"So, you see that failure to assimilate the Tubare's knowledge as subversion?" asked Zeke. "If what you say is true, you're only going to get a few rich people this way, and there is always somebody in the wings waiting to take their place. I fail to see how you think this is interesting, especially since it requires that you get chopped up."

The déjà vu energy was beginning to fade and his head was pounding as it always did after the retreat, like a hangover, but this one was the mother of all hangovers. He felt like throwing up. He felt like some portion of himself had melted a little and would never reconstitute, but he also felt vast, like the space his skin encompassed was beyond calculation. He felt that if he went much further south, given his assumption about the increased strength of these experiences and that direction, future experiences might kill him, or maybe leave him comatose, alive but not, a husk.

A strange look was in Wounded Man's face, one Zeke could not quite read: conspiratorial, but devious and accusatory too. When he spoke his tone was strange as well, half a suggestion this was a joke but deadly serious simultaneously.

196

"Imagine what could happen if he doesn't lose his mind. Imagine what could happen if he manages to assimilate that Tubare liver's knowledge within his *Norteño* context. Imagine a gringo warrior who knew that rocks breathe, a millennium to inhale and a millennium to exhale, that birds are messengers, that the death-dealing, omnivorous civilization into which he was born is doomed...at the very least our inevitable heathen revolution might be hastened from the inside."

****

If Strauss had indeed seen the last two Tubares, there was apparently only one left now. Wounded Man said that was who the man standing on one leg and leaning on a staff in the trail ahead of them was, the last Tubare. Wounded Man knew him by how he wore his hair, cut bluntly at jaw length, and by his loincloth-like wrap made of stripped bark.

The man balanced, like a big wading-bird, against a long smooth stick like the one Wounded Man had made for Zeke over their brief lunch break a few hours before. The foot he was not using rested against the inside of his opposite knee.

Wounded Man attempted to speak to the Tubare in a language Zeke had never heard, the Tarahumara tongue perhaps. The Tubare didn't seem to understand it either, or if he did he made no sign. He just stared in their direction as Wounded Man jabbered away at him.

Then the man walked toward them, slowly, solemnly. He acted like Wounded Man wasn't there, even though he continued to speak the language Zeke didn't know a word of even as the Tubare brushed by him. The Tubare stood in front of Zeke and stroked his chin as if thinking. His eyes were filled with something wild and immeasurable that Zeke knew he had never seen in anyone's eyes before, maybe a kind of knowing that was almost gone from the world, maybe loneliness on a scale he could not fathom. He was,

197

after all, the last. Wounded Man watched the Tubare in silence now. The next move seemed to be his.

"What is in a man who is the very last of his kind?" asked Zeke aloud after a few minutes of no sound but bird noises and the wind high in the trees. It was a rhetorical question. A question posed to the air. A question without an answer, or so he thought.

"Grief mostly," said the man in concise English like the Jesuits teach, "and the fear I will forget something before I die that some better man could at least carry to his grave. The way my father walked or my wife sang or my friend Tewa snored only under the new moon or where the trail on a given ridge leads or how to turn tree bark into clothing or into tea or the noise a jaguar makes when it sneezes or the fact that jaguar is also Tepegollotli, 'the heart of the mountain,' and our ancient connection to the most ancient peoples or how to make a trap to catch birds or how to stalk geese by swimming under them or what stars the Gods steer by or the smell of a woman's sex that is like dirt after rain but also like blood or the gait of a she-wolf in heat or the songs for sunrise and for hunting and for the birth of children and for the magician who has lost his way or which one is the moon's good eye or which wind is good luck and which one ill or what streams hold the beasts who-pull-you-down or how old stones are or how many teeth yellow squirrels have or how they became yellow when the sun spit upon them or the seven attributes of love and which four are positive and which three are negative or the sound the heart makes when it is hungry or the time I failed to be a good man in my despair or the secret wealth of ravens or the power in their stale breath or their mother the night who spawned them and her admonition that makes them dangerous and makes them the keepers of the bottom of the world or how pine smells in the morning or the prayer of mourning which I can never forget because I say it daily or the cure for sleeplessness and cough that is in the roots of century plants but only when they are blooming or the names of stars or the eloquence of certain birds...."

198

The Tubare spoke for hours, staring into Zeke's eyes as if he were transferring this information through them, as Zeke stared back, transfixed, and with an overwhelming perception of arrival, of having achieved a place that required the entire universe to align just so in order that he could arrive where he now stood, as Wounded Man sat as witness near them.

The Tubare talked until dusk and then on into the dark. Zeke stared into his eyes and then into the dark space where the Tubare's eyes were after it was too much night to see them, then into his eyes again when the full moon rose over the trees to the east, then into the dark space after the moon passed beyond the treetops to the west.

When the birds began to sing again just before dawn, the Tubare ceased talking. He walked silently around Zeke, who stared straight ahead at the spot where the Indian had been, and the last Tubare disappeared into the trees.

Chapter 31

After Cindy returned from Mexico, she learned something about fame in America, not its Warhol-esque lack of breadth, but its Warhol-esque lack of depth, the sad relationship of message to commodity and both to the evaporative nature of fame.

Immediately upon her return to Denver, after sending Kalish into fits of spastic laughter with her account of cosmic coincidence, she summoned Jonny Quarrels to her apartment and showed him the pictures of the bowels of the Prison of Serpents. He explained the complexities of international law to her, the absence of much beyond diplomatic mechanisms to influence judicial decisions in other sovereign nations before a verdict, let alone after the fact as in Zig's case, empathized with her over the appalling conditions, and then Cindy bopped him squarely on his square attorney's chin.

The lawyer picked himself up off the floor with tears in his eyes and consternation in his voice, but Cindy wouldn't allow him to speak beyond his first few faltering words.

"Wake up, Jonny Quarrels," she said. "I pay you for your abilities in this regard, not for your sympathetic ear or bullshit excuses. This is the age of the indispensable lawyer, isn't it? Now, do whatever it is an indispensable lawyer must do to make this right."

So Jonny Q. put Cindy in contact with a friend of his from college who was now an administrator at PBS, who put her in contact with an in-house director who, as quickly as possible, after Cindy insisted stridently through the administrator through Jonny, who lost sleep over the initial fragility of the arrangement and because his jaw still ached, made a half hour documentary featuring the photographs and shots of a camera crew being turned away from the gates of the prison by none other than *El Comandante* Frederico Fernandez himself.

Within days of the broadcast the networks aired knock-off versions of the story for their news magazine programs. Two of them used the pictures and Cindy's eyewitness testimony, and all of them interviewed other Americans with loved ones in Mexican jails, mostly for drug offenses.

There were also gallery showings in Denver and New York. The pictures were blown up to life-size: all piss-pails and iron bars and thin men in rags bathed in the stark light of hell. An aesthetic of horror, one reviewer called it. A triumphant testimony to human suffering, said another.

Cindy was a much sought after interview as well. She told her story to the New York Times and the Washington Post and Newsweek and to the two major Denver dailies. They all printed her photo next to some of the pictures she and Zig had taken in the prison. The captions to the latter read: Americans in Hell and The

Inhumanity of Man and The Penalties for Drugs May Be Larger than You Think. The captions under Cindy's photo, because she had been recognized from her ad by a surprising number of correspondents, all male, tended to be a play on words: Phone Sex Queen Seduces the Truth out of Mexican Prison System, Phone Sex Star Nails Mexican Officials, and Phone Porn Entrepreneur Lays it on the Line about Mexican Jails. Cindy Sweet Stuff's phone sex service did record business three weeks running because of the pervasive publicity. Apparently not all who read the articles were interested in prison reform.

The general American public, however, was appalled at prison conditions in Mexico, outraged, vehemently pissed, boisterous in their protestation, writing letters to Washington and even marching in the street a few times. Then they weren't. Quick as that. Their attention had been captured by a seal named Sigmund in the Washington Zoo who could whistle "Dixie" and the theme to Star Wars simultaneously. Most Americans couldn't separate the two songs and had to admit the creature's music sounded like a tune born of chaos theory, but expert musicologists had been flown in and verified that all the notes were certainly there to those two songs. Amazing, said one TV anchor. Incredible, said her partner.

"But worst of all," Cindy told Jonny Quarrels, "the PBS program and two of the network segments were brought to the American public by one of the largest insurance companies in the country, and the same corporation that owns the insurance company is the largest private contractor of prison systems in the world.

"In fact, I got a call from someone at Amnesty International who asked if I knew that the PBS film was being used now as a marketing tool."

Cindy had to pause. She had wept all night, not out of despair but a sense of violation, and for the impoverished communal soul of America. She had a lump in her throat again, but her sadness had transubstantiated to rage. Jonny Quarrels moved to comfort her, but decided against it when he saw the same look in her eye as was there just before she punched him.

"Apparently," she continued, "the insurance company has convinced PBS that their motives in underwriting the story were, and remain, the humane treatment of prisoners worldwide, and PBS has relinquished all rights to the film.

"Now the corporation has hired F.F. himself, former District *Federale* Commander and Warden of the Prison of Serpents, to show the videotape to officials in Central and South American capitals, to demonstrate the inconvenience of their old barbaric ways, to sell them stackable concrete boxes with stainless steel bars and lidless stainless steel toilets and a drain hole in the floor for easy cleaning."

Chapter 32

Wounded Man suggested that they rest a few hours, then resume. He had scouted back the way they'd come a few miles, looking for any sign that Dominguez and the bounty hunters were close and had found nothing.

"But that doesn't mean they're not there. Dominguez is very good at not being seen." Since he had slept off and on during the Tubare's recitation, Wounded Man said he would take the watch while Zeke slept.

For a while Zeke slept like a dead man curled around the trunk of an ancient pine just off the game trail they'd been walking when they met the Tubare. When he realized the man was no longer in front of him, Zeke had collapsed directly in the trail in a heap. He was exhausted, but the exhaustion was good, like that after athletic sex or after the first meal to end a fast. Wounded Man had said something about Zeke being chosen, and used a string of profane adjectives before calling him a gringo almost tenderly, as he helped him off the trail; but Zeke was too nearly asleep to hear him completely, too filled with something unspeakable to care. He felt like he had been filled to the brim and then some with something unnamable, or perhaps that was made of so many names he might burst with all the details he held, like he now had a great responsibility he could neither shirk nor fulfill.

Then Marianne's face, complete with its singular wound, appeared in his dreams. She made her usual peculiar motion with her mouth to whistle, her lips puckered and her gapped front teeth framed by her lips and her tongue sticking out just a little and protruding upward a short way into the space between them, but words came out instead of music, contrapuntally. Each word was followed immediately by its own echo a few steps higher in pitch. The effect was strangely melodic, but unsettling.

"You are the Diaspora of a dying race," she said, "but the Indian just told you the parable of your animal virtue. Your own cultural heritage may be highlighted by soft drink jingles, machines assigned human qualities they can't possibly really have, and the perverse desire to transmogrify into a meat-byproduct, but you have a far greater need now because of what he told you...learn something here, Einstein."

Then Marianne's face moved back and forth in Zeke's imagination, faster and faster until all her features, including her wound, blurred to an image of colors flowing together. Then her face stopped, but it was a cat's face now, wild and big with eyes like the Tubare's eyes.

Then Zeke was inside the eyes, watching himself sleeping, curled at the base of the large tree. The sunlight was brilliant. Everything, his body and the trees and Wounded Man with his back turned several yards away where he watched the trail and the abundant undergrowth and the detritus becoming dirt on the forest floor, glowed. Everything radiated its own particular version of light. The trees were brighter than the ground, the undergrowth was a deep somnambulant hue, and Wounded Man was a vibrant

203

hum of multiple colors; but Zeke's own body where he slept was strangest: a soft blue glow surrounded it, but that color was tinged with red around its edges, a purplish crimson like old blood. Zeke knew any interpretation of symbolism was irrelevant. There was meaning in those colors, but he didn't yet have the context within which to decipher it.

All he knew at this point with absolute certainty was that the world before him was a swarm of objects, of infinite substance, a tactile feast; but the world was also ceaseless movement, miraculous action, a sensational oscillation and spinning of everything. Everything had a smell too, strident and in flux, but an odor irrevocably its own.

He knew fear, akin to the fear he felt under the stars years ago in Iowa but bigger, and an odd exhilaration, a confidence he could not have imagined existed. Like God must feel, he thought.

And in the center of it all was a bewildered man, sleeping. His edges were blurring, faltering as if he were melting into the final earth. The smell of confusion and fear rose from that body, blue and tinged with red, like mist from a pond.

Zeke padded softly into the trees, feeling strength like incipient, barely sleeping lightning in his new body. He felt wildly alone. He could smell men on the wind, and evil, and death.

Chapter 33

Cindy could not sleep. Jonny Quarrels breathed loudly beside her, deep in the ludicrously sound sleep of an overly tired child or of a man without conscience. She had told him never again, but what the hell....

She received a note from Strauss weeks before saying Zeke was on the move again, this time deep into the wilderness to escape the bounty hunters who had roughed her up at the Howard

Johnson's in San Ignacio. There were hints in the anthropologist's prose of a new threat too, something worse than a couple of reprobates with shotguns, more dangerous than the prospect of prison, but Strauss was obviously purposefully vague, perhaps to avoid the bounty hunters or the authorities from finding out much if they intercepted the note. The peculiar tone of the thing only served to heighten her anxiety.

Cindy had hired a private investigator to search for Zeke, but so far he hadn't even managed to find Strauss. She suspected her searcher spent his time drinking in one of the cantinas on her money or had found a girlfriend in San Ignacio. He urged patience when he called that morning, and hinted he was looking for a guide to take him into the Sierras or that he might hire a plane in Mexico City to hop over them so he could check out a few of the towns on the other side, but Cindy was losing faith in his abilities. For all Strauss' attempt to veil the new risk to Zeke in his letter, Cindy was more certain than ever that his life was imminently in danger.

"Patience, my ass," she had said to her private investigator before she hung up on him.

She intended to leave in the morning to look for Zeke herself. She was going to the Prison of Serpents one more time anyway, to give the new *Comandante* money for Zig's release. She had been in contact with him, and he had named his price, a pathetically low price for a human life, she thought, a few thousand dollars.

She had already bought Zig a house two doors down from the one he promised her before his fateful trip. That house had been purchased by a Catholic couple, a cop and a parole officer, who had seven children. Zig had always wanted kids he had told her when he proposed. Now he could help raise these, and the proximity of their parents could help keep him out of further trouble with the law, hopefully.

Cindy had also bought Zig a new Harley to replace the one the Mexican authorities confiscated, and she was playing with the idea of bringing him into the phone sex business. He would need a job, but she still wasn't sure if women would call such a service, since the sexual dynamic was different for them than for men. Women would at least need the whole thing contextualized differently, rather than Safeway carts in public they'd expect it over the dryer with the phone man who writes poetry in his spare time maybe. She would have to think some more about the theoretical possibilities, and, besides, she fully realized she didn't know Zig well enough to tell whether or not he was trainable. Taking good photos inside a prison was one thing, and talking nonstop about little to nothing phone sex quite another.

Jonny Quarrels was suing the insurance company/prison contractor for copyright infringement on her behalf, because her deal with PBS was for one time rights only, but he'd warned her that a corporation with such large assets would definitely hit her with a countersuit of some kind and the whole mess would probably last for years. She had been adamant that they proceed whatever the odds. Amnesty International had offered to pick up a small, symbolic portion of the legal fees, which made their chances at least appear a little closer to even, though Cindy had no illusions about the prospect of winning. She wanted to make her point, she told Jonny, and if they could eat up a chunk of those "assets" in the process so much the better.

Jonny Q. wasn't complaining. Cindy paid him well for his services, and the Amnesty International lawyers were also actively recruiting him for a high profile case in Arizona involving a former academic being held without bond for allegedly making threats against the president. Jonny had admitted to Cindy that he was considering it. "Think of the PR," he said.

The man in Arizona had become something of a cult figure in recent weeks, giving long erudite press conferences from jail, imploring Americans to "pull their heads out of their fat collective ass" in Rolling Stone, publishing 10,000 word tracts about the subtleties of cooptive manipulation under late capitalism composed completely in long manic, Whitman-esque lines.

Based on her own flirtation with fame and trying to make a point in public, Cindy feared this guy would go the way of all cult figures and get swallowed up by it all...and in the end, in spite of his message, travel America making speeches to hero-worshippers who would pay him for his presence, for being their hero merely because they need one so badly...or, like her, he would be utterly forgotten and so would his cause, his own words used perversely by the opposition to prove their point. She sent money to his defense fund anyway.

She tried to sleep again, but Zeke returned to her as a memory regardless of her attempts to dislodge him with all those other thoughts and plans and memories, to dislodge him with mundane, attorney sex. After all she had been through, her irrational response to this one man made less sense now than ever.

She was not really so much saddened by his absence as she was perplexed at how she felt about his absence. She knew she must hunt for him, that either he needed her in some existential way, literally in order to survive, or that she needed him, that her path to purpose lay in his direction. He had, after all albeit in a roundabout way, been the reason she found Zig. And Kalish insists Zeke is still in her future, at least she assumed the old woman was referring to Zeke. Damn that old lady and her cryptic evasion anyway, she thought.

Cindy walked naked from the bedroom to the room she called her office when she worked on the books or advertising or scripts for the phone sex service at home. She called Kalish and got her out of bed.

"Alright, old woman," she said without identifying herself, "the guy headed south with a piece of me in his heart is part of my puzzle, and a bigger part than you ever let on given recent events. What does he have to do with the tundra-sparrow-sized stain on my soul?"

Kalish, yawned, or sighed, Cindy could not tell which. "Your love-stars must be aligned with his," she said, and then was silent for several seconds before she burst into laughter.

"Very funny, old lady," said Cindy. "False astrologies aside, and by the way I'm still not sure that everything you've told me isn't of the same charlatan variety...give me a straight answer, just this once."

"The answer is the same as it was before," said Kalish, and there was more than a hint of anger in her voice. "Figure it out. You're an absurdly strong woman for one of your race. Quit pretending otherwise."

Cindy waited in the dark, naked but not cold, for the travel agency to open. She would book a flight south. She would find Zeke. She would slap fate hard to see what fell out of its mouth, rotted teeth or diamonds.

Chapter 34

Royalty, sovereignty, power, fertility, earth, night, the spirit realm...Zeke was the embodiment of these things. Zeke was these things, and he knew names he had never heard before, even from the last Tubare: Tezcatlipoca, Lord-of-the-smoking-mirror, Night-wind, Warrior, He-to-whom-we-are-slaves, Protector-of-magicians, Omnipresent-and-invisible-god-of-shadows-who-foretells-the-future-and-looks-into-people's-hearts, He-who-brings-bravery-and-riches-and-good-fortune-but-also-death-and-misery, and at least a thousand more.

Zeke knew that he was born because Ometecutli and Omeciuatl made love on the sands of the Mexican desert, because they made love on the verdant hills of Central and South America, because they made love in the dark Amazon. He was born curer,

Hunter, Lord-of-the-darkness, Traveler-in-the-underworld-from-west-to east, Eater-of-flesh, because of their divine sex.

He walked in this guise now: as darkness, as war, as death. He was bloody purpose wrapped in muscle and bone and skin. He was Tezcatlipoca himself and would look for all eternity, as he had looked for millennia, for his famous siblings: Huitzilpochtli of the Aztecs and Quetzalcoatl of the Toltecs and Xipe Totec who ruled over the first world epoch. They were born when he was born and vengeance fell to him for their defeat and banishment, for their dismemberment that was his dismemberment also, for the desecration.

Zeke knew beyond the shadow of a doubt that this was the beginning of the last age of man, that all beginnings are blood-stained and sad beyond imagination; but he also knew that before long he would be called on to be a curer, to be royalty and fertility and the-reader-of-fortunes-that-are-at-least-part-blessing. In the south. Always further to the south. Where his tale would certainly grow stranger still as he lived out the cosmic inevitability that was his duty within a story that began "before the beginning," as the Tubare had said, the story of the light and the dark locked in desire, locked in battle, forever and ever, Amen.

Zeke awoke under the tall trees of the Sierra Madre Occidental blood spattered and weary but far less bewildered than ever before in his life. He wondered where Cindy was right now, this minute. He imagined her naked in the dark, waiting for the sun to rise, a magnificent queen for a jaguar king, his omen, the singular blessing he would be allowed on this journey-to-serve-the-world, his love.

About the Author

MICHAEL MCIRVIN was born in the Nebraska Panhandle in 1956. He taught writing and literature for many years at various institutions, including Colorado State University and the University of Wyoming, and for the past several years he has been a freelance editor and writing mentor. His poems, stories, essays, and book reviews have appeared in hundreds of periodicals, and he is the author of nine books: poetry collections, novels, and an essay collection. He lives on the High Plains of Wyoming with his wife Sharon and is currently writing another novel.

Books by Michael McIrvin

Hearing Voices (poetry)

Optimism Blues: Poems Selected and New (poetry)

The Book of Allegory (poetry)

Dog (poetry)

Lessons of Radical Finitude (poetry)

Love and Myth (poetry)

The Blue Man Dreams the End of Time (novel)

Déjà vu and the Phone Sex Queen (novel)

Whither American Poetry (essays)

www.ingramcontent.com/pod-product-compliance
Lightning Source LLC
Chambersburg PA
CBHW071907220626
47052CB00002B/247